TIME OUT

TIME OUT

David Hill

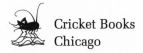

Cricket Books
Chicago

First published in New Zealand by Mallinson Rendel Publishers Ltd.

Copyright © 1999, 2001 by David Hill
Printed in the United States of America
Designed by Anthony Jacobson

Library of Congress Cataloging-in-Publication Data

Hill, David, 1942-
    Time out / David Hill.— 1st American ed.
        p. cm.
    Summary: Alienated at school and troubled by his parents'
separation, Kit loses himself in running, until one day an accident on
the road catapults him into what seems to be a parallel universe.
    ISBN 0-8126-2899-3 (cloth)
    [1. Coma—Fiction. 2. Running—Fiction. 3. Schools—Fiction.]   I.
Title.
    PZ7.H5489 Ti 2001
    [Fic]—dc21

                                            2001028870

With special thanks to:
Tessa Gould, Charlotte Gray, Danise O'Sullivan
and her Sacred Heart class

TIME OUT

Kit sprinted again as he crossed the last paddock. He swung himself over the stile between its two marker poles, pushed up the slope, and saw the school buildings ahead. Crowds of kids stood there, watching. Three seconds after Kit appeared, the cheering started.

They weren't cheering him. They were cheering Mark Taylor, behind him. Kit had been twenty metres ahead at that last paddock, but he knew he'd need all his lead. Mark was big and powerful.

And popular. Kit could make out voices from the crowd now. "Go, Mark! Beat the Geek!"

He didn't look round. He lowered his hands so his body bent forward more and let his bony legs swing. He'd hear Mark coming. He had enough strength left if he needed a final sprint. He was going to win.

He'd run the race just as he planned—staying back at the start while others pushed and jostled, breathing deep and steady so he got his second wind fast. Then he'd swept past Mark on the hill, where he knew the burly boy would struggle. Mark had stared at him like a startled goldfish. Principal Dudley, supervising that part of the course, looked more like a startled flounder.

Kit crossed the finish line, slowing down. He kept his face expressionless; didn't look at anyone. It didn't matter—hardly anyone was looking at him. They were all watching behind him, cheering, "Go, Mark! Come on, Mark!"

One spectator pushed past as Kit began his cooldown routine, lifting up his legs, walking around to help his muscles and heart return to normal. "Big hero, eh?" the boy sneered. Kit ignored him.

Big? he thought. Get serious. Mr. "Puni"verse, kids called him. He looked down at his skinny legs. He glanced back at the muscular figure now surrounded by admirers, especially girl admirers. Anyone would think the school cross-country winner was Mark Taylor.

Kit blinked as two faces appeared in front of him. A boy and girl in running gear, still panting from the race.

The girl smiled. "You were awesome! Taylor didn't know what hit him!"

Kit blinked again and tried to remember her name. Girls never talked to him. He opened his mouth, but no sound came.

"We've gotta have you in the team, man!" The boy was grinning, too. Hell, thought Kit, I can't remember his name, either!

The girl (Anna, was it?) spoke again, still heaving for breath. "There's this new girl—coming to school—she runs. Be an amazing team—with you two in it."

Kit dropped his eyes as she smiled at him again. They moved off, the girl close beside the boy.

"You were lucky," a different girl grunted at Kit.

"Yeah," said another. "Mark should have beaten you, boy."

Kit ignored them, too. Then, as he headed for the gym and his clothes, a voice spoke his name. A brisk, no-nonsense voice. Kit groaned silently. The school PE teacher was striding towards him.

Mr. Harris didn't look pleased. "You could have told us," he grumbled. "How long have you been running?"

Kit looked at the ground. "Couple of years. Just for myself."

Mr. Harris didn't *sound* pleased, either. "Just for yourself is pretty selfish. The school team needs you."

The silence that followed was broken by the teacher. "Well? How about it?"

Kit shrugged. A few more seconds, and he heard Mr. Harris sigh. "Look, son. I know your folks—I know there are problems at home. But you've got to get a life, eh? Think about it."

The PE teacher strode away. Kit kept moving towards the gym. Behind him, kids were still congratulating Mark Taylor.

• • • • • • • • • • • • • • • • • •

Science was Kit's first lesson for the afternoon. Miss Garden showed them a video to finish off their astronomy unit. Galaxies, each containing billions of worlds. Huge red stars, a thousand times bigger than the sun, exploding in clouds of dust and flame that drifted through space to form other suns and planets. There's so much in the universe that people know nothing about, Kit thought.

He liked Miss Garden. If *she* were the PE teacher, then he just might join . . .

She stopped him as the class began shouldering noisily out of the room. "Well done this morning, Kit. You made a few people think." Kit managed a half smile before his eyes went down.

"You liked that book I lent you," Miss Garden went on. "Want to try this one? It's about black holes and parallel universes and suchlike. Answered a few questions for me."

Kit took the book. Today was Friday; he could do with something to keep his mind off the weekend. He knew what *it* would be like.

Nobody spoke to him as he left the school. He moved alone through the yelling, chattering kids all planning their Saturdays and Sundays. Nobody seemed to see him.

That suited him fine. Maybe he could be Mr. Invisible as well as Mr. Puniverse. A faint smile lifted his mouth at the thought.

The smile faded as he passed through the school gate. His mother would be at home. What was she going to be like today?

Two

She'd been pretty much as he expected, Kit thought on Saturday—a still, hot Saturday with a haze growing along the horizon.

She'd kissed him when he got home. The sweet smell of sherry was on her breath.

"How did the cross-country go?" His mother's eyes were bright. She's had a few, Kit realised.

"OK," he muttered.

"Well?" his mother demanded. "Tell me!"

"I won."

"That's wonderful! Well done, dear!" She kissed him again. As soon as he could, Kit escaped to his room.

At dinner, he asked, "Dad rung today?" His mother's face went heavy, and Kit wished he could suck back his words.

"No. He's probably too busy with that fancy new girlfriend of his." She left the room. A minute later, Kit heard a glass clink in the kitchen.

• • • • • • • • • • • • • • • • • •

Chapter Two

His dad rang that evening. Kit and his mum were sitting and reading—and sipping, in his mother's case—when the call came.

Kit picked up the phone. There were voices talking and laughing in the background. A party? Parties seemed to start wherever his father went. Everybody liked him. Kit knew his mother still did, deep down.

"That's great, son!" his father exclaimed, when Kit told him about Friday's race. "They'll be wanting you in the school team, eh?"

Kit mumbled some reply. But he felt good. His father did that to people, made them feel interesting and alive.

His dad wanted to talk to his mother. Kit pretended to read about black holes again. He tried not to listen as his mum's voice became too bright.

He knew his parents worried about him. They couldn't last thirty minutes without an argument now, but they tried to put on a front, for his sake. He usually went away and left them to it.

About three months back, he'd heard them talking. They were thinking of giving him a holiday with friends—neighbours when Kit was little, an older couple who still signed themselves *Auntie and Uncle* on their Christmas card.

Kit wasn't sure how he felt. He wouldn't mind being in a house where people loved each other without hurting each other. But he didn't like leaving his parents. In the end, nothing happened.

His mother hung up and came back to her seat and glass.

"Your dad's coming over tomorrow afternoon." She tried to say it casually, but Kit could hear the tremble in her voice. Suddenly he ached to hug her. But he didn't seem able to hug anyone anymore.

Three

On Sunday afternoon, Kit went running.

His father's visit had turned out just like the other ones. For half an hour, the three of them sat and drank coffee and talked. His mum and dad even smiled at each other a couple of times. A silly hope started to build inside Kit.

Then—"Thought you'd have rung on Friday," his mother said suddenly. "It was a special day for Kit."

His father's face went watchful, but he stayed polite. "Fridays are always busy."

"You had enough time to find a party. With your girlfriend, I suppose." Kit heard his mother's voice shake.

"And you had enough time to half-empty the sherry bottle."

Before his father finished, Kit was on his feet and striding out. In his room, he stood and stared at the wall for a second. He snatched Miss Garden's book from his bed and flung it into a corner. Then he grabbed his running gear and began changing.

At the letterbox Kit turned right, heading up the narrow black ribbon of Jackson Road. The ditches on either side were full of daisies and pale grass, stirring in the warm breeze.

He began settling into his running rhythm, legs striding easily, arms relaxed and slightly away from his chest so they wouldn't interfere with breathing. He edged closer to the side as a car swept past, sending a cuff of air at him.

Jackson Road stretched silent in the summer heat. The slap of his running shoes on the black-top, the pattering of sheep hurrying away in a paddock, the rasp of his breathing were all Kit could hear.

He liked running by himself. It wasn't lonely. It brought him a feeling that was almost happiness.

Except when he got nagged about it. Before the cross-country, kids had reckoned he was weird. Now that he'd beaten their hero Mark Taylor, and then turned down the chance to be in the school team, they'd reckon he was more weird. They could think what they liked.

He was starting to hurt now. His lungs burned. The fronts of his thighs ached and his arms were growing heavy.

Kit didn't worry. It always happened about fifteen minutes into a run. He'd just let his mind float, put his body on automatic. Another few minutes, and he'd feel he was running through a silent tunnel, a private world where everything else seemed shadowy and unimportant. He could run down that tunnel forever.

He swung around a corner, across a peeling white concrete bridge, and into the long straight where Jackson Road aimed at the hazy horizon.

His skinny legs swept on. His mother worried about his being too thin. He didn't care.

Clouds were growing along the horizon ahead. White, black, purple towers of them, building and rising in slow motion.

He'd seen lots of such cloud-towers in the last few weeks. They rose during the hot summer afternoons, sometimes standing huge and silent till night came, sometimes slamming and echoing with thunder. Today's were the biggest and blackest he'd seen. Maybe he'd get wet. He didn't care about that, either.

His feet padded on. Post-and-wire fences and paddocks of freshly mown hay flowed backwards on either side. A concrete water tank, a cattlestop, a driveway between parched hedges.

A humming grew behind him, swelled into a snarl, and a pickup truck flashed past, so close that Kit swerved onto the rough roadside grass. A thick arm waved.

Kit kept his eyes down. He did it all the time at school. And at home with his mother. He went through life keeping his eyes down.

Four

His eyes stayed down now as he loped on. The blacktop ribboned past under his feet. The tunnel feeling was stronger. Beside and ahead, everything was shadowy. His legs and chest hurt; his back ran with sweat. But it all seemed distant.

He thought of Mark Taylor. Must have been the thick arm waving from the truck that reminded him. Mark was built like a bus shelter, but surprisingly quick. Those kids were right—another few seconds on Friday and he would have caught Kit. He remembered everyone cheering for Mark. Everyone except those two—hell, *what* were their names? They'd seemed really pleased Kit had won.

He thought, too, of what he'd read last night in Miss Garden's book—black holes, giant stars collapsing inwards till nothing could escape from their gravity, sucking in whole worlds that came too close.

Nobody knew what happened to anything pulled into a black hole. It vanished forever. Astronomers reckoned such holes might lead to one of those parallel universes. Awesome idea, Kit thought, as he strode past more hay-filled paddocks.

Maybe there was a universe where his parents were happy together. Anger at his mother and father flooded him suddenly. He clenched his fists, felt his face contort, his breath catch. The slapping of his shoes on the road was jerky and uneven.

You stupid sod! he told himself. Just run. Run forever.

A change of road surface under his feet made him look up. He saw a bend ahead, with the black-top narrowing as it curved between straggly thorn hedges.

And he saw the cloud.

A half shout burst from him. He lurched towards the middle of the road.

The row of cloud-towers still stood along the horizon in front, higher and darker now. But they were dwarves beside the huge, black shape swelling from their midst.

It was like a mountain, or a great, dark wall. It filled half the sky, black and vast and silent. The noises of sheep and birds from the paddocks around had stopped. The warm summer light was fading. The whole world began to darken.

Kit's feet kept carrying him towards the bend between the thorn hedges. Hedges that were shadowy now, as the gigantic cloud grew still higher and blacker.

A shape was forming in the blackness. A slow, spiralling shape like a great, dark whirlpool turning. Or the mouth of a cave leading into nothingness. Kit felt a prickling, a tingling that spread through his body like electricity.

Then the cloud roared at him.

It was a snarling roar that switched to a shriek. Kit reeled and ducked, throwing up one arm against the noise and the terrible black cave.

As he ducked, he suddenly saw. The pickup truck that had passed him before, now hurtling around the corner towards him, where he stood in the middle of the road. Its engine revved; brakes screamed; a horn blared wildly. A face stared from behind the windscreen. Hands wrenched at the steering wheel.

Kit flung himself sideways. One foot twisted on some loose stones. Then he was flying, diving through the air, arms and legs flailing as he tried to avoid the skidding pickup.

His heart had stopped. His eyes bulged. Above him, he glimpsed the cloud. The huge, black opening spun faster; it began plunging down over him.

There was another roaring, inside his head this time. A bellowing sound, like some giant animal. A wall of wind lifted and flung him. Road, paddocks spun dizzily and vanished.

From a great distance, a voice called "Kit!" It was his mother. His father seemed to echo her.

Then the enormous black cloud-mouth was on him. The summer sunlight shrank, rushed to a tiny point like the picture on a switched-off TV, and disappeared. There was silence and darkness and nothing else, ever again.

Five

He was staring at a daisy. An ordinary white-and-yellow daisy.

He was staring at his own hands, too. They gripped the top wire of a fence. He stood with one foot on a lower wire, looking down. The daisy grew beside his foot. He moved his running shoe and saw more of them.

A voice spoke his name. Not his mother or his father: a boy's voice, impatient. "Kitt?" it said again. It pronounced his name differently, as if there were an extra letter at the end. Kitt.

Kit stayed still for another second. He was alive, standing in his running gear, leaning on the paddock fence. The cloud—he glanced upwards—the great black cloud had gone.

"Hey, Kitt? Come on, eh?" Again the different pronunciation of his name. Kit straightened up. He took a deep breath and turned around.

The pickup truck had also gone. Stupid idiot, Kit thought. Hope a cop gets him.

Instead of the truck, five kids stood there. Two were guys; three were girls. All wore running gear: shorts and pale green singlets. A woman, also in running gear, stood behind them.

It was the closest girl that Kit found himself staring at. She was taller and thinner than the others. Her coppery-red hair was pulled back behind her ears and fastened with a clip. Sensible for running, Kit thought. Green eyes watched him, puzzled.

Kit realised he was staring into those eyes. Hell, he never looked at girls like that! Quickly, he glanced at the other kids. They had pale skin and brown hair. There were no dark heads like his, and no other redheads like the tall girl.

The same boy's voice spoke. "Who's in front now, Ms. Gorton?" The speaker was shortish, and vaguely familiar.

Gorton sounded like Kit's science teacher, Miss Garden. This woman looked different, though. Except when she turned her head . . .

"Alrika, I think." The woman nodded towards the bony girl. "And Kitt. You OK, Kitt?"

"I . . . wha . . . yeah." Kit realised he was moving towards the girl Alrika, as she stepped back onto the road.

Even as he joined her, his breath stopped again. His T-shirt had vanished. He wore a pale green singlet, just like the others.

They ran back down Jackson Road, Kit's legs moving

automatically while he fought to understand.

He was the same, except for the way he'd stared at that girl—Alrika. And except for the singlet he was wearing.

His body was the same, too. He was OK. He'd missed the truck completely. He put on a burst of speed to test himself, pulling away from the others.

"Hey, Superfeet! It's not—sprint training!" the third boy called.

Alrika drew level with him again. Kit saw sweat on her forehead and on the smooth skin of her neck, where damp curls of copper-coloured hair clung. He looked away a second time.

"Just follow—the training plan." The green eyes shot him another puzzled look, then switched back to the road.

What training plan? Who were these kids? What were they—?

As he ran on beside the girl, feet smacking and pattering behind them, Kit tried to take one thing at a time.

It was the same Jackson Road. The paddocks of hay hadn't changed, though he didn't remember those tall yellow-leaved trees, or that letterbox shaped like a drum. The sky . . . Kit looked again. Yeah, the great dark cloud had disappeared. Only a few white streaks marked the horizon.

He must have blacked out when he landed on the roadside. That was it; he'd got such a fright that he must have stood up again and been leaning on the fence before he knew. That explained it. Except for the other kids and Ms. . . . Ms. Gorton. Nothing explained them.

Kit turned his head once more to look at the others. Were they actually there? Had he dreamed them up?

"Try not to move your head around, Kitt." Ms. Gorton pronounced his name with that strange double *t* at the end. Kit glimpsed her, loping easily at the back of the group. "It makes you run crooked. You lose your rhythm."

The woman's breathing was even. She's fit, Kit realised, as she spoke again.

"I know it's all new to you. Best if you sightsee after training, though."

New was only half the truth. This must be a trick. Kids from the school, setting him up. He opened his mouth to ask what the hell was going on.

One of the other girls spoke first. "How we doing—for time? Don't want—to keep Mr. Nasser waiting."

"Don't worry," Ms. Gorton laughed. "Kitt won't miss science. Not in his first week. Don't step too long, Streve. You'll pull a muscle."

"OK." It was the shortish boy. The one who'd spoken to Kit first, the one who looked familiar. He was Streve.

No! He was Steve! *That* was the guy's name— the one after Friday's cross-country, the only guy at school who didn't treat him like a weirdo. Steve Sutton. And the girl running beside him was . . . not Anna . . . Hannah! Hannah Wesley. But they looked different now. Different, yet the same.

And Mr. Nasser—his name sounded like Mr. Harris. But Mr. Harris was a PE teacher, and this Mr. Nasser taught science. And—and Miss Garden at his school was the science teacher, while the Ms. Gorton now running beside him must be PE. Their names and jobs had shifted, somehow.

Then he understood. *Everything's* shifted. This isn't my world. This isn't my universe.

Six

For a second, Kit thought he would fall. He lurched in shock, veered towards the roadside.

"You OK?" the bony Alrika grunted beside him. And, as Kit managed to nod, "Come on, then!"

Irritation glowed inside Kit. He strode out over the blacktop. Alrika struggled to keep up, but she stayed at his elbow.

They came around a corner and over a weird-looking steel bridge Kit had never seen before. A long straight lay ahead, with a sprawl of familiar green-and-white buildings at the end.

"OK!" called Ms. Gorton. Straight away, Alrika was running harder, pulling away from Kit. He was startled for a moment, then he surged after her. The others' feet thudded behind; the warm air blew past his face.

A road sign drew closer. *Jackson Road*, at least that was the same. But the sign read *Jakson Road*.

At the same moment, Kit saw why the buildings ahead were familiar. They were his school. But his school shouldn't be here; it was on the other side of town.

What was here in his normal world? Kit tried to think, while the other kids stood around him, panting. That's right: the electronics factory. And where was his house? He hadn't seen it as they ran back.

He half caught Alrika's eye. The bony girl breathed deeply but didn't seem too beat. Kit remembered how he'd had to sprint to catch her.

Ms. Gorton (hell, he was thinking of her as a real teacher) looked pleased.

"Good. You're pretty fit. Just as well. See you tomorrow, then. And remember—only three weeks!"

Three weeks of what? Kit wondered. The girls had headed off in one direction, Streve/Steve and the second guy in another. Kit hesitated, then followed the two boys. He and Alrika were the tallest and skinniest by quite a bit, he noticed.

Of course—the boys were headed for the gym changing room. It was just like his real school's. Three sets of clothes lay on the benches: green-and-black track suits, quite cool-looking. His name was sewn onto one set. Not quite his name: *KITT*, the nametags read.

"Coming to science?" Streve asked. The other boy had left. "Mr. Nasser's good, eh?"

Kit grunted. He and Streve crossed the concrete playground towards the science block. It was exactly where the science block was in Kit's real school. "Real," he thought. This one seems pretty real.

Mr. Nasser was like Mr. Harris, all right. He didn't look the same, but when he moved and spoke, the resemblance was there. Except he seemed friendlier.

He grinned at the boys. "Good run?"

As Streve replied and Kit mumbled, the teacher went on. "This work might be new stuff for you, Kitt. Tell me if it is."

"Thanks, Mr. Harris." There were a few chuckles, and Kit realised what he'd said.

Mr. Nasser frowned at the chucklers. "That'll do. I'd like to see you lot cope the way Kitt's having to."

Kit tried to take in the last sentence as he headed for the only empty seat. The lesson was on atoms and what they were made of. It was old stuff for Kit, not new stuff. He was able to sit and think.

Had he imagined the cloud? No, it was real—like the pickup truck that had nearly hit him. He shivered as he remembered them both.

Then . . . was the cloud some sort of black hole? Had he been pulled into it? That was too weird for words.

He gazed around, wondering why he didn't feel more scared. The guy Streve sat a few desks away, whispering to the girl who looked like Hannah Wesley. Everyone here looked like someone from his other school.

Except for Alrika. The lanky girl was on the other side of the room. As Kit looked, her head went down over her book. Had she just been watching him?

Alrika didn't remind him of anyone. As Kit decided this, two words flicked through his mind like words on a flipped-over page. Not Yet.

"Mr. Nasser?" The Hannah-like girl was speaking. "You say there are these gaps inside every atom—between the electrons and nucleus and that. What if everything inside an atom got squashed up really close?"

The teacher nodded. "Good question, Hanni. Scientists reckon it happens. You know how?"

Hannah (Hanni?) looked blank. Kit felt his stomach tighten. He knew what was coming.

"It's probably the most amazing event in the universe. A star suddenly collapses in on itself. Its atoms squeeze together. The electrons inside them squash against the nucleus. It takes only a few seconds. The whole thing collapses into a black hole."

Mr. Nasser's final words brought murmurs of recognition. Streve's hand went up.

"If that happened to a planet, with people on it. Would they—"

"Would they survive? Well, for the Earth to become a black hole, it would have to collapse till it was just the size of a marble."

Murmurs of astonishment this time. "No," Mr. Nasser continued. "Nothing can survive in a black hole."

Seven

But I have, Kit told himself an hour later. I've survived. I'm here—wherever "here" is.

He was walking along a footpath with Streve. The shorter boy seemed to take it for granted they would go home this way.

Kit listened while Streve talked. Now he understood a few things. There was a cross-country race against another school—Rygel or some mad name—in three weeks. Each school had three pairs of runners, boy and girl. He was paired with Alrika, Streve with Hannah—no, Hanni. Kit didn't like to ask the names of the other two, but he felt he knew them, also.

"See ya, then," Streve said suddenly.

Kit stared at the house outside which they'd stopped. It was his parents' house. His parents' house exactly, but in a street he'd never seen.

Streve grinned at him. "Finding your way around? It's a long way from home, eh?"

Kit knew he must look like a mugged frog. But Streve didn't seem to notice. "How's the host family?" he asked.

Host family. Again, Kit felt his stomach tighten. "OK," he mumbled.

"Mum reckons they're cool," Streve said. "OK, see ya tomorrow. Gonna be a tough training, I reckon."

"What day's tomorrow?" Kit spoke before he could stop himself.

"Tuesday, of course. Why?"

"Just checking. See ya." Kit started up the path. After a second, he heard Streve move off. So today's Monday, he thought. It was Sunday when I started running. I've lost a day. And maybe a universe.

His heart seemed to swell as he neared the front door. Even the black door knocker was the same. Should he knock? Should he walk straight in?

The door opened, and there stood two strangers.

Strangers, yet Kit had seen them somewhere.

"Hello, Kitt." The woman gave his hand a squeeze. "Uncle Gil thought he heard you."

The man smiled. "Put my ears and your Aunt Fran's eyes together, and we'd have a superhuman."

"Come and have something to eat." The woman bustled towards the kitchen. "How did school go? Settling in?"

As Kit hesitated, the man whispered, "Your parents are still trying to get through, son. It takes time."

"How was training?" the woman called. "The school's thrilled you're in the team. I met Hanni's mother in the supermarket. Hanni says you're their best chance to beat Rygel."

Kit made himself say something. "It was OK . . . Aunt Fran."

The woman returned with cake and juice. "Come on. Help yourself."

The cake was brilliant—heavy and chewy and chocolate, like ones he remembered having when he was little. But Kit could hardly eat. His stomach felt heavy. His head throbbed. His hands had started shaking; he clenched them into fists.

Aunt Fran chattered about her shopping, Hanni's mother, how they'd accidentally walked off with each other's trolleys. Kit tried to listen and think. He was aware of Uncle Gil watching.

After a while, there was silence. Then Uncle Gil spoke. "Feeling homesick, son?"

Kit couldn't speak, couldn't look up. He nodded.

"Why not rest?" The man's voice was gentle. "We'll call you when dinner's ready."

"Yes, Kitt dear." Aunt Fran pronounced his name with the double *t*, also. "You must be so tired. A rest will help."

Kit felt as if a haze were growing around him. His head and body ached. Getting up from the table was a huge effort.

His bedroom was exactly the same. The astronomy book lay in the corner, where he'd thrown it before he set out for his run.

Kit looked at the book. He closed the door quietly behind him. Then he dropped across the bed and cried as if he would never stop.

He didn't know how long he lay there, face buried in the pillow to muffle his sobs. Whatever had kept him going for the last few hours had crumbled. Everyone he loved was gone. He was alone forever.

The haze he'd felt before seemed to be spreading over his body, into his mind. A faint beeping noise grew, then faded. The haze darkened, flowing into the shape of the huge cloud-tunnel. Kit let himself drift. The cloud was too enormous to fight.

"Kit!" The name sounded short and strangely clipped. "Kit!" He jerked—it was his father's voice. His mother joined in. "Kit! Hold on!" Then his father again. "Hold on, son! Hold on!" The cloud dimmed, ebbed away.

Kit lifted his head. The room was empty. He picked up the astronomy book. It fell open at a passage he'd read . . . was it last night or a whole existence ago?

If an astronaut took a shortcut through a black hole, he'd be stretched into spaghetti by its gravity. Or squashed into meatballs. Or fried in the great blaze of starlight that may be trapped inside the black hole's boundary.

I'm not fried, Kit told himself. I'm not meatballs. He glanced down at his skinny body. I'm not spaghetti—not quite. Mr. Nasser was wrong. He'd survived. And he . . . he was gonna hold on.

He straightened the crumpled bed. He went to the unchanged bathroom and washed his face. Later, when Aunt Fran called him, he went through to dinner.

Eight

Kit hardly slept that night. His mind whirled. Questions pushed and tugged at him.

Where was he? Where were his mum and dad? Who were these other people? His *host family*—was he on some overseas trip and he'd forgotten months or years of his life?

The bedside clock showed 1:38 A.M. Kit turned on his bedside lamp and picked up the astronomy book.

Since light stays trapped inside a black hole, unsquashed astronauts who have been inside the hole for an hour might see the light waves that show them entering the hole. They might also see the light waves of themselves an hour ahead. Their pasts, presents, and futures could all be trapped inside the black hole.

Kit put the book down. He turned out his lamp and shut his eyes. As he did so, a voice called. It was far away, at the very edge of the world. "Hold on! Hold on!"

Kit's eyes flicked open, and he lay staring into darkness. For a few seconds, the beeping noise sounded distantly. A little later, he felt himself sliding into sleep.

MACMILLAN SCHOOL. He hadn't even seen the sign yesterday, Kit realised, as he arrived in his green-and-black track suit next morning. The name meant nothing. Or did it?

Tuesday. He wondered where his missing day was. A bell rang, and everyone began moving towards assembly. "Hi," said Streve, appearing on one side. "Hi," said Hanni, appearing on the other side. Kit saw the boy and girl smile at each other, then blush. Hello, he thought. That's just like . . .

Assembly was like his other school—boring. But one notice made Kit sit up. "Training for the cross-country team last period. Meet Ms. Gorton at the gym."

The principal—a woman; that was different—gazed down the hall. "We all know how important this cross-country will be for Macmillan School. We wish our team and its new member good luck."

Kids turned and grinned at Kit. He didn't know where to look.

As he and Streve and Hanni came out of the hall, the principal strode past. "Hi, people."

"Hi, Mrs. Hedley," replied Hanni and Streve.

Mrs. Hedley, Kit thought. My other principal was Mr. Dudley. Somehow he knew everyone here. Except he hadn't seen Mark Taylor, the big hero. And there was Alrika. He didn't know her at all.

Streve sighed. "Be stink if Rygel win, boy."

"They think they're so cool," Hanni agreed. "Kitt's gonna give them a shock, though."

She smiled at Kit. To his amazement, Kit found himself smiling back.

In English, his class was doing video skills; in geography, they were studying how an oil refinery worked. Kit could handle it OK.

He couldn't handle the lunch Aunt Fran had made him, though. Filled roll, homemade cookies, yogurt, fruit—it was excellent, but he wasn't hungry.

In science, Mr. Nasser talked about anti-matter.

"There may be parallel universes made from different kinds of atoms. They'd be like shadow universes. If our matter and their anti-matter ever touched, there could be an explosion that would change everything."

Shadow universes, thought Kit. I wonder . . .

On the other side of the room, Alrika sat writing. Once again, Kit felt sure she'd been watching him.

Streve and Hanni were talking to Ms. Gorton outside the gym as Kit arrived.

"Hi, Kitt," the PE teacher smiled. "Hi, Mara and Connell."

Kit turned. The other boy and girl were approaching.

Mara and Connell. His parents were Myree and Colin. These two kids were his parents, years younger. They didn't look the same, but Connell's loud jokey voice and Mara's shyness—Kit knew them.

There was a pattern. A pattern he had to understand. If he could understand it, something might happen.

They changed into their white shorts and green singlets. Ms. Gorton led them through five minutes of stretches—swinging arms, lifting knees to chins, pulling feet up behind.

"The Rygel sports captain's coming tomorrow to check the course," she said.

"Better get it vacuumed first." Connell grinned, and suddenly looked just like Kit's father.

"Stride lengths," their coach added when they were stretched. "Some of you are trying to take big steps like Daddy Long Legs here." She smiled at Kit. "But short strides mean better balance—very important on a cross-country. OK, two warmup laps around the field. In your pairs. Talk to each other."

Streve and Hanni and Mara and Connell set off, chatting as they ran. Kit heard Hanni's giggle. He heard Connell's laugh. He glanced sideways at Alrika as she and he broke into a jog. Her thin face stared ahead. She stayed silent.

"Good science lesson," Kit said, after they'd run half a lap without speaking. Alrika shrugged.

Another wordless hundred metres. Kit felt annoyance grow again. "What's so important about this race?" he demanded.

The green eyes stared at him. Kit began to look away, then held their gaze.

"If Rygel wins—" Alrika hesitated. "If they win, there probably won't be a Macmillan School anymore."

Nine

For the rest of training, Kit was too busy to ask anything else.

As they finished their jog, he saw Ms. Gorton setting up hurdles on the field. He hated hurdles. He was scared of tripping over them and hurting his legs.

"You have to jump banks and things in the cross-country," the coach told them. "Hurdles are good practice."

Groans from Hanni and Connell. They hate them, too, Kit thought. I . . . I'm gonna try!

"Don't go too high," Ms. Gorton said. "It breaks your rhythm when you land. Just clear the top."

Streve and Hanni managed, awkwardly. So did Mara, who shot an anxious glance at her partner, and Connell. "Lower!" urged Ms. Gorton.

Kit shortened his stride. To his surprise, he cleared the top cleanly. Behind him, Alrika jumped. Thwack! The girl stood, rubbing one shin.

"Try shorter steps." Kit spoke before he knew it.

Alrika strode back to the start, then sprinted up again. Kit saw her lean legs shorten stride. She rose, flashed over the hurdle, ran smoothly on.

"Good, Alrika!" Ms. Gorton called. She winked at Kit and murmured, "And good, Alrika's partner!"

They spent half an hour hurdling. Kit's skinny legs sent him sailing over. I can do it! he told himself.

They spent ten minutes hopping. Hopping like fit frogs on both feet. Hopping like damaged frogs on one foot. "Balance training!" Ms. Gorton called. "Fitness!"

Finally, she sent her sweating, panting team off for three laps of the field. "Push yourself! Make it hurt!"

It hurt. Breath rasped. Lungs and legs ached. But Kit felt marvellous. He could run forever.

Connell and Streve finished first. Kit could have beaten them, but he was happy to come in next. Alrika was close behind him, bony arms pumping.

Kit glanced at her. He saw long smooth legs as she bent over, gasping for breath, pale face flushed with effort. He realised he was staring, turned quickly away, and fell over a hurdle.

Alrika watched him scramble up. "Try shorter steps," she suggested.

Ms. Gorton handed them a typed sheet as training finished. "Runner's diet. Show it to your folks. Heaps of carbohydrates."

"Bananas, parsnips, apples," Connell protested. "Only monkeys eat this stuff!"

"Eek-eek-eek!" went Hanni and Streve together.

During dinner that night, Kit asked about what Alrika had said—no more Macmillan School.

He asked partly to stop Aunt Fran from worrying about his not eating. Dinner was choice—vegetables stir-fried with strips of meat—but he had no appetite.

Uncle Gil nodded. "It's bad. Schools compete at sports, science fairs, everything. It's all to get sponsors. Mrs. Hedley hates it, but the government doesn't give schools enough money. Without sponsors, Macmillan could be finished. They hope the cross-country will bring some."

Kit remembered his father talking about such ideas. His father had liked them.

"Your folks want to make contact, son." Uncle Gil murmured as Kit left the table. "They do. Give them time."

In his bedroom, door closed behind him, Kit hesitated, then spoke aloud.

"Mum. Dad." He stopped, took a breath. "I'll hold on. I promise." He expected to feel stupid; in fact he felt better.

He read some of the astronomy book. It brought him closer to his world; he could picture Miss Garden lending it to him.

Do we really exist? he read. *Or are we just part of a programme in some giant computer?*

So maybe I'm here because someone pressed the DELETE key? Kit thought. He looked up at the ceiling, stuck his tongue out, crossed his eyes, and gave the finger to nobody in particular.

Now he felt stupid. And better still.

He slept longer that night. Once he woke to hear the beeping noise. Voices he knew seemed to be moving away from him.

Must have been Uncle Gil and Aunt Fran. Or maybe the computer owner was checking his programme.

Streve met him next morning as Kit came out onto the footpath, feeling guilty because he'd eaten so little of Aunt Fran's breakfast.

"Hiya, Kitt." Hell, thought Kit. I've got a friend!

"That Rygel guy's coming to work out a course with Ms. Gorton today." Streve sniffed as Macmillan School came into sight. "Jeez, I hope we waste them! They think they're so awesome. I'm glad you didn't decide to go there."

I didn't *decide* to go anywhere, Kit thought. He muttered something.

Streve grinned at him. "How are you finding Alrika? She's weird, eh? She can run, though."

A spark of mischief glowed inside Kit. "How are *you* finding Hanni?"

Streve's face turned pink. With his brownish hair, he looked like a badly designed sunset.

Then he pointed. "Hey, there's someone from Rygel! Must be their sports captain."

A figure was coming the other way. A figure in long black pants and a dark red jersey, walking confidently, ignoring the Macmillan kids. He turned into the school driveway.

"Big hero!" Streve muttered. "Acts like they've won the race already."

Kit stood still, watching the Rygel uniform. The tough, springy walk; the big shoulders. It was Mark Taylor.

Ten

"**Notice for our** cross-country team," Mrs. Hedley announced in assembly. "Meet Ms. Gorton at the gym, morning interval."

Geography first lesson: more oil wells. Then Kit, Hanni, and Streve made their way to the gym. Connell and Mara were already there. So was Ms. Gorton, with the broad-shouldered Rygel boy.

"This is Marec," the Macmillan teacher said. "We've been working out a course for the race."

Marec, thought Kit. It fits.

The boy—Mark/Marec—nodded. "He's cute," Kit heard Hanni whisper to Mara, who shot Connell another nervous look. Alrika arrived and watched without expression.

"Just wanted to wish you guys good luck." The Rygel sports captain looked at Kit. "Hi. Heard about you. Hope you enjoy running here."

Kit began to stare at the ground. Then he lifted his head, and gazed back at the boy in the red jersey. "Thanks. Hope you enjoy it, too."

A puzzled look flickered across Marec's face. "See you in about two weeks, then," he told the group.

In English, they were set a descriptive paragraph to write for homework: *How I Feel about My Home.* Alrika's copper-red hair fell away from her neck as she bent to copy the title. Wonder what sort of place she lives in, Kit thought.

Training began with stretches. Then a slow jog over the course Ms. Gorton and Marec had chosen. "Get to know it," their coach urged. "It's *our* course, *our* advantage."

They went across the playing field, down a slope, and over paddocks. A pine plantation, a couple of creeks. "Don't look for stepping stones!" Ms. Gorton told Hanni and Connell, as they complained about wet feet. "Go straight through."

More paddocks. A gravel farm track that looped back towards the school. Pines again, then out into the open, with a last paddock and a steep slope ahead. The roofs of Macmillan School showed at the top.

There were groans from everyone except Alrika and Kit as they saw the slope. "In the race, you sprint this paddock!" Ms. Gorton said. "You have to be in front before that hill."

Kit hardly heard her. He was staring ahead. The slope was exactly the same as the one up to his house.

. . . .

After the jog, they had a sprint relay in their pairs. "Across the field, back, tag your partner's hand. Watch how they run. Tell them at the end."

The three girls went first. Alrika was slower on the turn than Hanni and Mara, but her long legs ate up the distance. She was half a metre in front as she tagged Kit. *Whacked* Kit; his palm tingled as he ran.

Behind him, Ms. Gorton called, "Touch hands, Hanni and Streve. Don't *hold* hands!"

Kit sprinted as hard as he could. He glimpsed the other boys catching him as he turned, felt himself draw clear again on the return run. Mara and Hanni bounced up and down, yelling at their partners. Alrika watched him silently. He strode across the line, still clearly ahead.

Comments time. "Lean forward more," Kit panted to Alrika. "Especially at turns. Use your long legs. Let them stride." He remembered staring at the girl yesterday, and looked down at his own skinny legs in embarrassment.

The girl's voice was level. "You need to keep your stride going. Keep your rhythm." She stopped for a second, then added, "Hold on."

Kit's head jerked up. Dizziness swept through him. Then other voices were in his mind—his mother and father, far away. "Hold on, Kit! Hold on!"

He staggered. Ms. Gorton grabbed his elbow. "You OK, Kitt?"

Kit mumbled a reply. The other kids stared. On Alrika's face was an expression that could have been fright, could have been understanding.

Uncle Gil was out that night. A meeting to discuss the future of Macmillan School. Aunt Fran and Kit ate dinner together—vegetable pie with lots of the parsnips on Ms. Gorton's sheet. Aunt Fran glanced at his hardly touched plate, began to speak, stopped.

In his room, Kit wrote his English assignment— *How I Feel about My Home*. He described the house on its hilltop, the views for miles. "It's a silent place, mostly," he watched himself write. "My host family here—Aunt and Uncle, I call them— talk and laugh a lot. But my mum and dad . . . "

He hesitated, began to cross the last words out, then went on. His hand was stiff when he finished. He suddenly felt drained. He called goodnight to Aunt Fran, and yawned his way to bed.

But sleep wouldn't come. He pictured again the moment on Jackson Road. The pickup truck tearing at him, his wild dive onto the roadside, the vast black cloud swooping down at him.

Kit shuddered at the memory. Something had changed forever back then. It wasn't just a different, green singlet. Or a different name and day, even a different world. Something still more huge had happened. He had to find it. He had to hold on.

Eleven

Next morning, he stood staring in the bath-room mirror. It was the first time he'd really looked at himself since things had changed. He'd been avoiding it.

The same dark hair, flopping over his forehead. The same brown eyes. The same cheeks, though the bones showed more. He was skinnier all over.

"You must eat!" Aunt Fran told him when he left his breakfast toast.

Uncle Gil changed the subject. "I told at last night's meeting that Macmillan will win the cross-country no problem, with you and Alrika running."

Kit saw his chance. "Is Alrika new at the school?"

"She's—" Aunt Fran stopped, looked surprised. "Funny—I thought I knew everyone in this place." Uncle Gil's face was puzzled, too.

Streve was waiting on the footpath. The two boys walked towards school, Streve complaining how they'd need rocket boosters for the last hill on the course.

"That Alrika," Kit said after a few moments. "She been here long?"

Streve frowned. "Yeah . . . no. Actually, she's—"

He stopped, an embarrassed grin on his face. Kit saw Hanni crossing the road ahead.

"Oh, hi," the girl said. "Thought I'd come this way today, for a change."

In spite of the worries crowding inside him, Kit smiled. He already knew that Hanni lived on the far side of the school.

She and Streve talked about training and their stiff legs from yesterday's sprints. Hanni reckoned an escalator would be better than rockets for the final hill. She told Kit that his host family were neat people and didn't seem to notice how his face changed.

I'm not a weirdo here, Kit thought, as they reached the main gate. I've got friends. I could be happy here, if . . .

"Kitt?" He had to read his English assignment on *How I Feel about My Home.*

He lowered his head and began. The words that had poured onto the paper last night came steadily. The great bowl of sky above the house. The clouds over far hills. One cloud filled his mind for a second. He heard his voice grow quieter, heard the hush in the room as he described Aunt Fran and Uncle Gil, and his parents.

When he finished, there were murmurs of "Awesome," and scattered clapping. Kit kept his head down a moment longer. Then he looked up, straight at one person watching from the far side of the room.

Alrika and he held each other's gaze for a long second. Then the girl nodded.

"A fortnight tomorrow." Ms. Gorton pointed to each of them as they warmed up at lunchtime. "That's all we've got."

"First we jog the course again," she went on. "We run it till we know it with our eyes shut— which is how you two seem to be running!" The coach glared at Streve and Hanni, who stood smiling at each other. Two faces turned pink.

Already, the course was forming into a pattern. The easy downhill stretch. Pine plantation and creeks. Paddocks and gravel road. More pines. The final paddock, and the slope angling up like a ramp to the finish.

"Watch the narrow bits," Ms. Gorton said as they ran. "Don't get caught behind anyone there."

Alrika loped along silently. Streve and Hanni were quiet, too, after the teacher's words. Connell wasn't quiet; he was cracking funnies all across the flat bits. Mara laughed, joked also, but glanced at the others. The faces of his mum and dad flicked before Kit's eyes.

"OK, a little surprise," Ms. Gorton announced when they finished the final slope. Even at a jog, its steepness had them puffing.

While the Macmillan team watched, their coach dragged a sack from the gym. Out of it, she lifted small hand weights and saggy, heavy-looking belts with Velcro straps.

"Aw, no!" Connell and Streve groaned.

"Aw, yeah," Ms. Gorton replied. "Weighted pads around your ankles; hold the hand weights. Go up the slope six times. Get up with these, and you'll fly up without them."

The next fifteen minutes were simple. Simple torture. The sand-filled ankle belts made it feel like struggling through an uphill swamp. The hand weights pulled them off balance, dragged their arms down.

No talking or joking now. Just gasping and grunting as they fought up the slope. Hair was plastered to necks. Sweat dripped from noses.

Connell and Streve struggled up together, with Hanni and Mara a long way behind. Alrika, bony jaw set, pushed herself upwards. Kit shortened his stride, watched the ground beneath his feet, wondered if his heart would explode.

And he felt great. He could sense the determination of the others, hear their grunts as they started upwards again. This was his team. He'd give heaps for them.

They sprawled on the grass at the top of the hill, sobbing for breath, feeling their hearts slow to normal speed.

"I'm dying!" groaned Hanni.

"I'm dead!" groaned Streve.

Kit struggled to a sitting position, head resting on pulled-up knees. Beside him, Alrika was doing the same, shoulders heaving.

Kit remembered the nod she'd given him in English. He turned to her.

"What you said yesterday—after those sprints . . . "

The girl's flushed face jerked to look at him. Kit felt nervous suddenly.

"You said *Hold on*. Do you—"

"I don't remember! I didn't mean anything!" Alrika twisted to her feet and hurried off towards the gym.

But Kit had seen her face. It held the same recognition as when he'd almost blacked out yesterday. And the same fear.

She knows something, he told himself. She knows.

Twelve

"No training tomorrow," Ms. Gorton told them as they creaked away towards the gym. "Special teachers' meeting."

In science, Mr. Nasser grinned an evil grin. "Here's a question to drive you mad. We've talked about black holes and other strange things that may exist. But does *anything* exist? Is anything really there when you're not thinking about it?"

Puzzled noises from the class. Alrika, who hadn't looked at Kit since training, lifted her head.

Mr. Nasser grinned again. He's friendlier than Mr. Harris, Kit thought. Or I'm seeing him differently.

"Take Streve as an example," the teacher said. "Can anyone prove he exists?"

Silence for a second. Then—"You can see him . . . You can hear him . . . You can *smell* him!"

Mr. Nasser joined the laughter. "But can you prove it? How do you know it's not just happening in your mind?"

More suggestions came quickly. "How about when you talk to someone? When you see things on TV?"

Their science teacher shook his head. "You still can't prove those people or the TV are really there. They could be part of some programme your mind is running, while you're awake or while you dream. Same with this discussion."

Another silence. Then Alrika's voice. "What about the past?"

"What about it?" Mr. Nasser replied.

"There's stuff written about the past." The girl's green eyes were fixed on her teacher. "We all remember things from the past."

Murmurs of agreement from the class. Mr. Nasser nodded.

"Good point, Alrika. But even the past could be dreamed up by your mind. Maybe there's nothing in the universe except a giant mind. Tough luck if it's Connell's mind, eh?"

Connell grinned hugely. Alrika was silent for the rest of the lesson. So was Kit. He felt tiny suddenly—as if something huge had begun moving slowly towards him.

He walked home by himself that afternoon. Streve just happened to be going in Hanni's direction.

Uncle Gil and Aunt Fran seemed tired. They said little. Dinner looked and tasted great once again—a hot salad with bacon and eggs mixed in.

Kit made himself eat some, but he left his plate half full. His stomach felt cold and shrunken.

He couldn't relax. Finally he announced he was going for a walk. "My legs are stiff from training." It was partly true.

Outside on the footpaths, the feeling of something moving closer was still there. It wasn't scary; it was just around him, like the ground and sky. Kit almost expected to see the great cloud rising above the horizon. But there was only blue-and-gold late sunlight. Daylight savings here, too; he snorted at the silliness of the thought.

Passing adults nodded to him. Some kids greeted him by name. Yeah, he could be happy in this world. He marvelled again at how calm he felt so much of the time.

But this wasn't his world. His world was with his mum and dad. Would he ever find it?

He didn't read the astronomy book that night. But he sat holding it in both hands for a while. He walked around the room, touching the corner of his bedside table, the wardrobe door, holding a pillow against his cheek. A sigh, or maybe a sob, came from him. Then he went to bed.

When he woke, his bedside clock read 12:16 A.M. The feeling was there again: something edging closer. He had a sudden picture of faces around him.

A car hummed past outside. Then the night

was quiet. Kit lay, feeling calmer. Whatever was happening, he couldn't do anything about it. After a few minutes, he felt himself sinking back into sleep.

There was something over his chest. No—over his whole body. He felt it as he came awake a second time. It was like a net, holding him, drawing him into darkness.

Voices murmured, too faint to hear properly. They faded, came back, faded once more. He couldn't move his arms or legs, but it didn't matter. Inside the net, he drifted towards the dark.

The distant voices murmured again. "—on," he heard. His mother's voice. And his father's. "Hold—" But it was too far away, and he was too tired. He floated, turning and sinking into the mouth of the black cloud as it rose now around him.

Then lights blazed. Green lights, sudden and terrible. Kit jerked. His whole body leaped in terror. He tried to yell, but his mouth was paralysed; no sound came.

The lights were eyes. Green eyes glaring. A face shouted at him. The words thundered inside his head. "Hold on! Hold—"

The darkness wavered and fled away. He was falling, hurtling downwards. All thoughts of drifting vanished. He twisted and struggled, trying to grab something.

The eyes glared, boring into him. The voice screamed in his head. "—on! Hold on!"

Then so suddenly that he heard himself cry out, the eyes were gone. Something pushed firm and solid against his back. He lay awake and panting in his bed.

Thirteen

An hour later, he still lay there, staring up at the ceiling.

His body felt dry. Dry and cold and heavy. And so weak that he could hardly move his head.

Kit pictured the face and the green eyes. Alrika. And not Alrika, the way that other people here were like and unlike the people he'd left behind.

Something hugely important had just happened. When the face glared at him and the voice yelled, a great choice had been made. The feeling of something moving towards him was gone. Or at any rate, it had retreated far away.

Alrika, he thought again. I'll ask . . . no, it's no use. She won't talk to me.

When Kit slept, it was his longest and deepest sleep since everything had changed.

He still wasn't hungry at breakfast. He scraped half his granola down the sink while Aunt Fran was out of the kitchen. Uncle Gil came in as Kit headed back to the table. He glanced at the now empty plate, and said nothing.

"You're allowed to talk, eh? It's Friday." Streve's words pricked Kit's silence as they neared the front gate of Macmillan School.

"Hey," the other boy went on. "I asked Mum and Dad about Alrika—you know, how long she's been here. They can't remember, either. Weird, eh? So's she."

Kit remembered the same being said about him. "She can run, though. Hey, where's Hanni? Thought she'd started coming this way?"

"I—she—hey, there's Connell and Mara! Wait up, you guys!" Streve gratefully headed off towards where Connell stood talking and Mara stood listening.

Kit began to follow, then stopped. Alrika was approaching.

The girl halted in front of him. There were light freckles scattered across her nose, Kit saw.

"Kit—" One *t*, not two. And it was the first time she'd spoken his name.

Alrika hesitated, started again. "There's this teachers' meeting at lunchtime, remember? You want to walk over the course? We've gotta have a race plan."

Kit saw the others watching. He saw also the awkwardness in the girl's face. "OK."

Alrika nodded. "Start from the gym," she said, and strode away on her long legs.

"How come she doesn't bite *your* head off?" Connell demanded, as he and the others joined Kit.

Kit shrugged. "Because I'm so handsome?"

Alrika was waiting for him outside the gym at lunch-time. As he came across the grass, Kit realised that for the first time in days, he felt hungry.

He had no time to think about it. "Come on," Alrika said, and strode off towards the downhill slope.

They were silent till they approached the first lot of pines. Then the skinny girl spoke.

"The first guy and girl home are almost sure to win for their team. We've got to stick together. No use one of us finishing way behind the other. You with me?"

Kit's face went hot, but he made himself speak calmly. "I'll try to keep up."

Alrika, striding into the pines, stopped and swung around. Kit found himself looking straight into her green eyes. He smelt soap and clean skin.

They gazed at each other for a moment, then looked away.

"We gotta be careful on that first downhill." The girl's voice was hurried. "There'll be lots of dorks going flat out and crashing into one another."

It made sense. "And we stick together through the trees," Kit added.

More silence as they moved on through the cool pines to the first stream. "Some of them are gonna try and find a narrow place to get across," Alrika said, as they stood on the bank. "We should go straight through. Surprise them."

They stood together, watching the hip-deep water. For a second, the copper-haired girl seemed about to speak again. Then she turned and headed upstream to where they could jump from boulder to boulder.

The girl's long legs carried her across easily. Kit followed. "Pity it's not a long-jump course," he said as they reached the far side.

Alrika stayed silent. For a second time, Kit's face felt hot. Was he carrying germs or something?

They were halfway along the gravel farm road, with the final slope starting to rise ahead, before the girl spoke again.

"I'm better on the flat than the hills. So we go really fast here, like Ms. Gorton said. Build up a lead."

Kit grunted. They walked on, through the second pines, over the paddocks to the last slope. It looked even steeper than when they'd struggled up with the weights.

"I'll follow you up here." As Kit began to reply, the girl jerked her head impatiently. "Listen! You're the strongest on the team here. You set the pace. I'll follow. Yell at me. Call me names. Make me keep up."

Now she looked at Kit. Her pale face was flushed. Her eyes glittered. For a second, Kit felt himself falling, just as he had last night.

"We have to win this, right?" The girl's gaze never faltered. "Because this race is gonna change everything. Isn't it?"

Fourteen

Kit expected the weekend to crawl past. It sprinted past instead.

Back home—he couldn't stop using the word—he spent weekends reading or running, staring out at the huge horizons and pretending not to notice when his mother tipped more sherry into her glass.

But here, people kept wanting him.

First he went to the supermarket with Aunt Fran. He went willingly, wondering if he might see Alrika.

Mr. Nasser was pushing a trolley down the aisles. He gave Kit a smile. So did some girls from his English class. There was no sign of Alrika.

But in the carpark, Kit saw someone else he recognised. Marec, the broad-shouldered Rygel sports captain, was talking to two girls, who gazed at him adoringly.

He saw Kit. "Hi. How's it going?"

"Pretty slow," Kit replied. Marec grinned. But all the way to Aunt Fran's car, Kit felt the eyes on his back.

Chapter Fourteen

He had a decent lunch. He was definitely hungrier. In the afternoon, he helped shift firewood into the garage. He felt safe somehow when Uncle Gil or Aunt Fran was near. It was like being with someone who'd known him forever.

As they finished the last barrowload, Uncle Gil spoke quietly. "Don't forget about your parents, Kit. Things will change."

Kit said nothing. But Thursday night's feeling that something huge had been decided rose again in him.

In bed on Saturday night, he opened the astronomy book at random. *There may be billions of parallel universes. Every time we choose a jacket, some other "we" may choose a different jacket in a different world. Every one of these universes will be partly the same, and partly different.*

Kit remembered Thursday's science lesson. So maybe this isn't Miss Garden's book at all, he thought—it's only in my mind. But he still felt better holding it.

Eyes closed, he saw the moment on Jackson Road, five—no, six days ago. The colossal cloud, the pickup truck and its bulky driver, his desperate leap for the roadside.

It didn't frighten him so much now. He stretched an arm out, touching the familiar wall, bedside table, and bedclothes as he'd done two nights ago. Then he slept, with no dreams.

He felt bad on Sunday. Sunday was when his father came to visit. What were his parents doing about him? Was another Kit living normally in their world, same as last week—or last year, however much time had passed there?

Just before lunchtime, the phone rang. "Wanna go to Connell's and watch a video?" Streve asked.

Kit ate lunch—more than he expected—while Aunt Fran beamed. He walked to Streve's place. A block further on, the two boys met Hanni and Mara, wandering in the same direction. "Connell asked if we wanted . . . " Mara began.

At home, Connell was more like Kit's father than ever—loud, cracking jokes, describing the video's scary bits while Mara and Hanni put their hands over their eyes and wouldn't watch.

But Kit enjoyed being with him and the others. I'm different now, he knew. I've changed. I'm gonna do things better when . . . if I get back.

He wondered where Alrika was. None of the others mentioned her, but he knew she was in their minds.

Fifteen

Kit made his way towards school on a dazzling Monday morning. His stomach was full of Aunt Fran's granola and toast. His ears were full of Streve's conversation.

"Did some weights last night," the other boy announced. "Squats, mostly. Building up my leg strength. It's OK for you; you've got nothing to carry!"

Kit glanced down at his own legs. He might be eating again, but they were still skinny.

"We've got a good team, eh?" Streve sounded embarrassed, but went on. "Even if we don't beat Rygel, it's cool being with you guys."

"What's the Rygel team like?" It was all Kit could think of to say.

Streve thought. "Marec's good—and he knows it. He's got a really strong finish. Dunno who his partner is, but their whole team's gonna be good. Rygel's got all these sports sponsorships. Big firms pay to have their names up at the school."

They walked on. "You and Alrika have got them thinking, though," Streve said. "Hanni says the Rygel kids keep asking about you."

Kit remembered Marec's look at the supermarket on Saturday. He remembered Mark Taylor not even bothering to look at him at his old school.

In assembly, Mrs. Hedley seemed to have her mind elsewhere. In science, Mr. Harris—no, Mr. Nasser—was edgy, too. He snapped at Streve for whispering to Hanni.

Miss Garden—Ms. Gorton; the names were mixed up in Kit's head today—also seemed tense when her team met by the gym. But she got them started quickly.

"Proper warmup, please." For five minutes, the six kids and their coach stretched muscles, held still for ten seconds, stretched further, relaxed, started again. Connell joked. Hanni and Streve talked. Mara listened and laughed. Kit and Alrika said nothing.

"OK," Ms. Gorton said. "Today you run the course in your pairs. Work out tactics, find how to get the best from each other."

Alrika looked at Kit. A half nod passed between them. Now we'll find out, Kit thought. Now we'll see if we're any good.

Keep out of trouble early on, Kit remembered, as he watched the other four bound down the slope, pushing and laughing. Alrika was in front of him.

She increased pace as they approached the first pines. Kit kept close behind. He could hear the others puffing already.

Out of the trees, across the open ground towards the streams. "Watch—your partner!" Ms. Gorton called, as Hanni and Streve, Mara and Connell scattered in different directions, looking for the easiest crossing.

Straight as an arrow, Alrika headed for the water. She slid down the bank, splashed through the hip-deep stream, bounded up the other side. Just five seconds, and they were fifteen metres ahead of the others. "Magic!" Ms. Gorton shouted from behind.

The second stream. Again Alrika went straight. Her feet slipped on the stones, and Kit grabbed her bony elbow. The girl pulled herself free and pushed on.

They reached the gravel road. Alrika lengthened stride, legs scissoring over the ground. We're miles ahead, Kit thought. Then he pictured the broad shoulders and confident face of the Rygel sports captain, and he increased his own speed, drawing level with Alrika. "Great—stuff!" he panted. The girl said nothing; her face was set.

Through the second lot of pines they went, out into the open for the last time. There was no sound of the other four; even Ms. Gorton's voice was well back.

The last slope rose in front of them. Again, Kit

thought of the hillside up to his parents' home.

He surged forward, taking the lead. As the ground angled upwards under his feet, he shortened stride, elbows thrusting.

"Head—down!" he grunted to the girl panting behind him. They battled up the hill, Kit listening for Alrika's feet. "Go!" he demanded silently. "Hang in! Hold on!"

The clumps of grass and the marks where people had slipped on previous runs jerked past. Then they were over the top, on the level ground beneath the wide bowl of sky.

We can do it faster still, Kit knew as they stood, hands on hips, gasping and staring at each other. Awesome!

Ms. Gorton was just nearing the top of the slope. Behind her, the others struggled upwards.

"Brilliant!" The teacher's face was flushed and excited. "You two have really been planning!" She patted Alrika's shoulder, and smiled at Kit.

Streve and Connell arrived, collapsing on the grass. Hanni and Mara were close behind.

"Awesome!" Streve gasped. "You're gonna show—those Rygel guys!"

"We'll all show them." Ms. Gorton smiled. "We're all going to work together like Kitt and Alrika." Kit glanced at the lanky girl. She was gazing at the ground.

"Those streams—" Hanni pushed hair back from her perspiring face. "I kept slipping."

Ms. Gorton nodded. "We have to watch the stones. OK, that was brilliant, people. Speed work tomorrow. Eleven days to go!"

Alrika was already heading for the gym. Connell nudged Kit with his shoulder, and grinned his easy, friendly grin. "You guys were amazing!"

"It was Alrika's idea," Kit told him. "She—"

His words faltered. Just twenty metres away, Alrika hesitated, started forward, stopped again. She stared up into the clear blue sky. Then she jerked backwards, pushing out her hands as if to keep something away.

"Al—" Hanni began.

The other girl stumbled. Her hands pushed out again. A croaking sound came from her throat. Her whole body shuddered, and she toppled sideways onto the ground.

Sixteen

Suddenly, Kit remembered himself tumbling away from the rushing truck. His own body jerked. Then he and the others were hurrying to where the girl lay hunched and trembling.

"Alrika?" voices gabbled. "What happened? You all right?"

A pale face stared upwards. Alrika's eyes focused on Kit. She mumbled something.

"Crowd?" Hanni looked puzzled. "What crowd?"

"*You* crowd!" Ms. Gorton pushed through. "Move back, eh? Give the poor thing some room."

Their coach knelt beside Alrika, who was struggling to sit up. "Take it easy, love. You overdid things, eh?"

"I'm—all right." Alrika stood, then staggered. Ms. Gorton and Mara grabbed her arms.

"No wonder you're wobbly, the way you went up that last hill." The teacher and the two other girls helped Alrika towards the gym.

"You OK?" Streve asked Kit. "You're not gonna faint in pairs, are you?"

Kit watched Alrika disappear into the gym. He knew what she'd mumbled. It wasn't *crowd*. It was *cloud.*

He ate a good dinner that night. Rice with vegetables, fresh fruit salad with heaps of bananas. Aunt Fran was pushing the carbohydrates into him.

But when he looked at himself in the bedroom mirror, he was startled again by his skinniness. And his colour: his skin was paler, as if he'd been indoors for a long time.

Kit gave his reflection a shrug. He knew it was no use worrying.

He knew something else, too. Tomorrow he was going to get the truth from Alrika.

But Alrika wasn't at school on Tuesday. Not in science, where Mr. Nasser talked about the great explosions that ended the lives of stars. Not in English, where they wrote about opposites *(Fast and Slow, Cold and Hot, Silence and Noise—also called Mara and Connell).*

Kit wrote about Pain and Pleasure. Fighting his way up the slope yesterday, heart banging, breath tearing, feeling agonised and awesome at the same time. Writing about it made him feel good again. I'll do more writing, he told himself, wherever—wherever and whoever I am.

"Nah, haven't heard anything," Hanni said at

training. Mara shook her head. Connell and Streve looked blank.

"If she's still away tomorrow, I'll ring her mother," Ms. Gorton said. Then she looked uncertain. "Or is it her stepmother?"

Tuesday's training was thirty metres jogging, thirty metres long-striding, thirty metres sprinting, another thirty metres jogging. The whole lot over again. And again.

"You need to be well ahead, Kitt." The double *t* was so familiar now that Kit hardly noticed it. He nodded as his coach went on.

"Marec's got the most powerful finish I've seen. He's a big guy; relies on his strength. You've got to build a lead so he can't catch you. What you two did yesterday was perfect."

Kit nodded again, and wiped his sweaty face on his green singlet. He missed Alrika's silent, edgy presence. He needed her there to make him run his best.

"Ten days," Ms. Gorton reminded them as they finished their last sprint, Connell and Streve powering in just ahead of Kit. "Then it's Rygel."

Rygel. Kit repeated it to himself. Why was the other school's name starting to sound like one he'd heard before?

Tuesday night's dinner tasted brilliant, too, but Kit couldn't eat much.

He felt tense again. As soon as he could, he escaped to his bedroom, the familiar place in a strange world. The astronomy book lay on a chair.

If you travel backwards in time, will you grow old before you reach the year you were born? Will you see a window break before the stone hits it? Will you see an author "start" on the last line of a book and write backwards, while ink vanishes off the page and up the ballpoint?

Thanks, but I've got enough problems already, Kit said silently. Then a knock sounded on his door.

Uncle Gil. He looked at Kit, then away, at the wall beside him.

Kit's hands clenched into fists. He's heard from Mum and Dad! They've gone. I'm never going to see them again. They're dead.

Seventeen

"Sorry to interrupt, son." The *son* made Kit's eyes prickle. "Just wanted to say your Aunt Fran's thrilled you're eating again. A change like you've had—it's a huge shock."

"Yeah." Kit wondered what the quietly-spoken man knew.

"You've probably heard how Mac-millan is having money problems?" As Uncle Gil spoke, Kit's fists unclenched. It wasn't his mum and dad.

"There's a big electronics firm in town," his host father went on. "They're tossing up whether to sponsor us or Rygel. I hear they're waiting to see who wins the cross-country."

He shook his head. "Everyone's going to be following the race now. But it's not your problem. OK, son?"

Kit nodded. Uncle Gil watched him. "If you could put it into words, Kitt, why do you run?"

Kit answered slowly. "It's not just the buzz. I—I find out things about myself.

And I feel . . . lucky. There are people who'll never run. They're in wheelchairs and that."

He stopped. Why hadn't he ever talked to his dad like this?

Uncle Gil picked up the astronomy book and started turning it over. "We're right behind you, Kitt. Aunt Fran and me. You're special to us."

He smiled at Kit and left, closing the door behind him.

Wednesday morning was blue and gold and calm. The weather's been perfect ever since things changed, Kit realised. Perfect and unchanging, as if the sky had stopped still.

Both Streve and Hanni were waiting at the corner. "Hope Alrika's back," were Hanni's first words.

"We need her, boy!" Streve agreed. "Only nine days left!"

There was no sign of the lanky girl in assembly. Mrs. Hedley surveyed the rows of pupils.

"You'll be aware of our teacher meetings. You may have heard about sponsorship decisions for the school." She looked along the silent faces. "Please don't worry. Macmillan School will always be a place where everyone matters, not just winners."

Kit had to read his *Pain and Pleasure* piece in English. Once again there were admiring murmurs when he finished.

He kept his face calm, but he felt himself glowing, the way he did when he ran. Writing and running, he thought. They *both* help me find out things. I'm going to run and write forever.

Connell and Mara crossed the grass towards the gym at lunchtime, ahead of Kit. They stopped suddenly and stared. Alrika stood by the gym door, Ms. Gorton beside her.

"You all right?" Mara's shy voice asked. At the same time, Connell's non-shy voice announced, "She's back! The fastest legs in town!"

Alrika, now bending over her running shoes to lace them up, said nothing. Kit glanced at her coppery curls and thin shoulders. He and she were the different-looking ones, all right.

There were more pleased noises as Hanni and Streve arrived and saw the bony girl. Then Ms. Gorton clapped her hands.

"Get changed. Tomorrow we do the course again—see if everyone else can think like Alrika and Kitt. Today you're really lucky; it's stamina training."

Groans from Streve, Hanni, Connell, and Mara. Ms. Gorton hurried them away. She's keeping attention off Alrika, Kit realised.

He was heading into the gym when he heard his name.

"Kit." The single *t*. He saw that Alrika's green eyes had a fleck of gold in them.

"We have to talk." As Kit stared, the girl hurried on. "Not yet. In a couple of days. Please?"

Then Ms. Gorton was back, bustling and ordering.

"Come on, people. Shake a leg! In fact, shake both legs. We're going up Jakson Road."

More groans from the changing rooms. Kit swallowed. Jakson Road, where they'd finished their run last Monday. Also called *Jackson* Road, where he'd started off from his parents' house, a few days or a whole life before. What was going to happen this time?

Eighteen

Nothing happened. Nothing, except that by the end of the run, everyone was totally beat.

They did their warmup stretches, while Alrika's words and thoughts of the run jostled in Kit's head. Then they headed off up Jakson Road.

It was just the same as nine days ago. The yellow-leaved trees, the paddocks, the letterbox like a drum.

And it was just as different from Jackson Road. The strange steel bridge instead of the white concrete one. Slopes where he half expected to see a drive leading up to his parents' house, but where trees grew instead.

The perfect blue sky curved overhead. The distant, lion-coloured hills glowed in the sunlight. Kit remembered the great tower-clouds rising above them and shivered.

Alrika loped along beside him, eyes on the ground. The others ran steadily. Kit could feel their concentration; the race against Rygel was starting to get to everyone.

A murmur grew behind them, became a buzz, then the roar of an engine. Kit's back crawled; he tried to keep his rhythm as he pictured the hurtling pickup truck. A blue car zipped past, with a wave from the driver. The others waved back, except for Alrika.

Kit thought of the bend ahead, where every-thing had changed for him. What would . . . but Ms. Gorton's voice broke in.

"Right, we'll turn around. Now you work in your pairs. One pair sprint to the front and stay there. When I say, next pair sprint to the front."

It sounded easy. It was exhausting. Sprint, keep running as the others overtook, sprint to pass them, keep running. Feet thudded, lungs heaved. After the first three sprints, Kit thought he was going to throw up. He saw Hanni stumble, and Streve grab her arm.

"Help—your partner!" Ms. Gorton called. Kit heard Connell grunt "Go!" to Mara, gasp "I'll lead!" as they raced past.

It was his and Alrika's turn to sprint. The girl's long legs moved out to pass the others. Nice legs, Kit noticed.

The two of them swept to the front. Suddenly Kit felt brilliant. His stomach had settled; his breathing was slower; his legs moved effortlessly. Sheer pleasure flooded through him. He grinned at Alrika.

The girl's eyes flickered. She smiled back, uncertainly. The first smile I've seen from her, Kit realised. Her bony face looked softer; little creases curved beside her mouth.

Hanni and Streve panted past, then Connell and Mara. The school's front drive was just ahead. "Sprint!" yelled Ms. Gorton. "Everybody!"

They finished in a gasping bunch by the drive entrance. "Marvellous!" beamed their coach, as she patted backs. She hesitated beside Alrika, then gave the skinny girl a hug. "We'll show Rygel!"

Kit ate a giant helping of Wednesday's dinner. Then he ate *two* giant helpings of dessert.

"Well!" smiled Aunt Fran as she refilled his plate. "You've changed!"

Yeah, thought Kit. I have.

There were voices in his dreams that night. Voices asking questions. The beeping noise sounded briefly. After a while, it faded into silence.

"Have you got room?" Aunt Fran exclaimed on Thursday morning as Kit buttered and honeyed a fourth piece of toast.

Uncle Gil appeared in the doorway. "Streve just rang. He can't meet you this morning; he has to pick some things up from Hanni's." His host father winked at Kit.

Kid after kid greeted Kit as he walked to school. "You're gonna win it for us, eh? . . . You should come and live here."

There was drama discussion in English and a lesson on volcanoes in geography. Yet again, the day was sunny and perfect.

"Yesterday tested your legs," Ms. Gorton told her six runners as they gathered by the gym at lunchtime. "Today tests your brains. Yes, Connell, it's hard to test what you don't have, but try."

Grins from various faces. Alrika, stretching and bending like the others, had her head turned away.

"Eight days till the race," their coach went on. "Today we run the course again. Look for the difficult bits. See if you can give the others any advice. OK, we're in business."

It was a good run. Kit could have gone faster. He knew the others could have, too. Everyone was watching instead—watching their partners and the course.

The other two pairs were about equal. Connell was strong but rushed ahead early, while Mara ran steadily but was awkward across the streams. Hanni was the slowest but good over obstacles. Streve had a fast finish but took a while to get going.

They were still close together when they came out of the second pines and headed across the paddocks towards the final slope. The other four had followed Alrika straight through the streams—with a few yelps and some stumbles on the stones. Kit knew the skinny girl was running well below full speed. And he knew that today she wanted to stay with the others.

As they reached the slope, she glanced over her shoulder. She moved aside, hissed "Now! Go!"

Instantly he burst forward, powering upwards. Alrika stayed with him; Kit glimpsed her from the corner of his eye. In twenty strides, the others were left behind.

"You should carry—tow ropes!" Hanni told them, as she struggled to the top.

And "Let me—grab your singlet—next time!" Connell complained.

Ms. Gorton meanwhile stood smiling. "Great stuff! You really look like a team."

Across from Kit, Alrika gave her coach a hesitant smile. Again, her face looked brighter and softer.

She's different, Kit knew. She's made up her mind about something.

Nineteen

Friday's training was talk. Nothing but talk.

"You're physically fit," Ms. Gorton said, as her team sat on benches inside the gym. "Are you *mentally* fit? Any hints for one another, like I asked yesterday?"

For ten minutes, they talked about Streve's too-slow starting, Connell's too-fast starting, Mara's stream-crossing, Hanni's lack of speed. There were comments, nods, careful listening.

"Kitt?" Ms. Gorton asked when it was his turn.

"Going really good," said Hanni. "Awesome finish on that hill."

More nods. Then Streve said, "He keeps looking round. Breaks his rhythm."

Kit pictured his other school; how he'd kept glancing around to avoid people. "Cool," he said now.

"Alrika?" their coach asked.

Connell's voice. "Great finish, too. Really goes for it."

Kit heard himself speak. "Could try and relax. Be less tense."

Murmurs of agreement. Alrika picked at her shoe.

"How about Rygel, Ms. Gorton?" asked Mara.

Their coach looked thoughtful. "They're confident. Some will start really fast. But Marec's the one to watch. He'll wait and go for a big finish."

"We should all go really hard across the stream." (Hell, thought Kit. Is this really me talking?) "Surprise them there."

He saw the determination on the other faces. A week from today, he thought. It's gonna be quite a time.

After her words on Wednesday, Kit kept expecting Alrika to say something to him. But she'd stayed silent.

No Marec at the supermarket on Saturday. No Mr. Nasser. As Kit and Aunt Fran started down the second aisle, however, they met Mrs. Hedley. Suppose even principals have to shop, Kit thought.

The two women chatted about the shocking price of groceries. Then, as she wheeled her trolley away, the Macmillan principal smiled at Kit.

"We're very proud of this young man. I wish he were one of ours permanently."

Aunt Fran was silent as she and Kit moved on.

He couldn't settle on Saturday afternoon. He tried to read. He wandered round his room. Finally, he went for a jog into the country, in a different direction from Jakson/Jackson Road.

Leaves were losing their bright summer green. Autumn wasn't far away. The world kept changing— whatever this world was.

Uncle Gil was waiting when he returned.

"Alrika rang." Kit seemed to see a half-wink flicker across his host father's face. "She wants you to call her back."

It was a man's voice that answered. A loud, unfriendly man's voice.

"What? Who? Hang on, will ya?"

Distant shouts in the same voice. Then another, cautious voice that Kit recognised. "Hello?"

"Hi. It's me—Kit."

"Oh. Hi." A pause. A noise which Kit realised was the girl taking a deep breath. "Can we walk over the cross-country course? Tomorrow?"

Kit felt puzzled. Then he understood the message behind the words. "Sure. In the morning?"

"Ten o'clock. At the gym." A click, and Kit was left with the humming receiver in his hand.

They watched a TV movie on Saturday night, after a dinner where Kit ate every scrap. During the ad breaks, he raided the fridge, while Aunt Fran looked pleased.

In bed, he picked up the astronomy book as usual.

Can time-travel change our future? Suppose you went back in time and accidentally shot your grandmother. Then you wouldn't have been born. But if you weren't born, you couldn't go back and shoot your grandmother. And if your grandmother wasn't shot, you would have been born.

Kit tried to understand, then gave up and went to the bathroom. There he tried to understand something else. Now that he was eating so much, why did he still look so skinny? And so pale?

Sunday morning's weather was still perfect.

Alrika stood waiting by the gym when Kit arrived just before ten. She wore white shorts and a black T-shirt that made her coppery hair glow.

They walked down the slope and through the first lot of pines in silence. She wants to talk, Kit decided. She can make the effort.

Alrika stopped by the first stream, staring down at the water hurrying over its stony bed. Kit waited a few metres away.

When the girl spoke, she kept her eyes on the stream.

"You been having dreams?"

The shouting face, the glaring green eyes, the falling, struggling feeling of Thursday night swept through Kit. He had to wait before replying. "Yeah. You?"

Alrika's gaze stayed on the water. "You weren't in them at first. I was running. Running and falling. There was something huge."

Kit stared. The girl swallowed, started again. "Then there was this big white place. My head and arm hurt. My mum was there. And you."

They picked their way across the streams on the stones. As they neared the second lot of pines, Kit spoke. "I feel like—like something's gonna happen soon."

Alrika kept walking. "Things are a real mess at home."

Kit didn't know where to look. Alrika moved on, among the cool, scented trees. "My mum tries. Her boyfriend—he's in jail half the time. He beats her up. I go running to get away from things."

Out of the pines, their feet scrunched on the gravel road. "I can be anybody I want when I'm running," Alrika said. She stopped, so suddenly that Kit almost banged into her. She stared at the final hill rising ahead. "That's where it's gonna happen, isn't it?"

Kit knew she meant more than the race. Hope and fear surged in him.

"You—when you blacked out last Monday. What happened?"

The girl spun to face him. Her green eyes were huge. "Nothing! You heard Ms. Gorton. I—I over-did things!" She turned and strode off.

They crossed the paddock and climbed the final hill in silence. She's lying again, Kit knew. She saw something.

Five days to go, Kit told himself as he walked home. Then . . .

The sky was no longer a perfect blue. Along the horizon, above the crinkled hills, a line of clouds was building.

Twenty

On Monday morning, the clouds hadn't moved. But they looked darker and thicker, packed above the hills.

"Be glad when this Friday's over," Streve greeted Kit. "Went for a run yesterday morning. Rang you, but you were out."

Kit made a neutral noise. He wasn't saying anything about Alrika.

"Connell knows one of the Rygel guys," Streve continued. "If they get this extra sponsorship, they're gonna build an all-weather athletics track. Haven't those dudes heard of grass?"

"You folks will all be able to watch the cross-country this Friday," Mrs. Hedley announced in assembly. A pleased murmur rippled through the hall.

"Rygel will have people here, too," the Macmillan principal went on. "Plus we're expecting a number of the public. I want you to welcome everyone politely."

So several kids bowed to Streve and Kit as they made their way to geography.

Monday's training began with hurdling. "Imagine it's the streams," urged Ms.

Gorton. "Lift your legs. Kitt was right—that's where we surprise Rygel."

Then it was sprinting up the last slope, with weights around ankles and in hands again. Alrika fought her way up behind Kit. "Go!" she hissed at him when he glanced over his shoulder. Otherwise she never spoke.

Nobody said much, not even Connell. "Four days to go," Ms. Gorton reminded them, as they sprawled at the top of the slope. "Four."

The phone rang after dinner on Monday night. Aunt Fran answered, looked annoyed.

"No, he doesn't, thank you." She put the receiver down.

"The local paper," she told Kit. "Asking how you feel about Friday's race, since it's so important. Sorry, dear, I should have checked if you wanted to talk to them."

Kit shook his head. "No way."

In bed that night, and again on Tuesday morning, he wondered. Maybe he was keeping things locked up, like Alrika. Maybe he should have poured everything out to Uncle Gil and Aunt Fran earlier on.

Too late—he'd made himself a different person in this place. On Friday he'd prove that. He wasn't going to mess this up.

"It takes you about thirty-five minutes to run the course," Ms. Gorton told her twitchy team on Tuesday. "You'll be puffing after ten minutes. Your legs will be hurting after twenty minutes. You'll reach that last slope after thirty minutes, and think you can't make it."

She paused. "So today we run for *forty* minutes. I call out the time; you tell yourself you can keep going."

They ran on the sports field. Round and round the sports field, leading in turn just as they had on the road.

Since Streve and Hanni were the slow starters, Ms. Gorton made them go fast early on. Since Connell liked to rush off, she yelled at him to stay back.

"Remember your partner!" she called. "Relax your arms, Alrika! Don't look round, Kitt!"

She's an awesome coach, Kit told himself. He remembered his thoughts about Miss Garden after the cross-country in his "real" world. If she were his coach . . . well, she *was* his coach, and he was in the team.

He jerked back to the present as he and Alrika swung out to take their turn in front. He glimpsed the pale skin and brown hair of the other kids, saw his own skinny legs, still somehow darker than the Macmillan runners'. Beside him, Alrika's bright coppery hair bounced on her neck.

Other Macmillan kids had come to look. Kit saw the guys among them watching when Mara and Hanni went past. And—yeah—when Alrika went past.

"Ten minutes . . . Twenty minutes . . . Thirty minutes." Ms. Gorton counted off the time. Kit hardly noticed. His body ran on like a machine. The aching in his chest, the sweat running down his neck seemed to belong to someone else.

They crossed the line for the last time in a bunch. They bent over, hands on hips, sucking in air. There were cheers and clapping from the spectators.

Once again their coach moved among them, patting shoulders and murmuring praise. "Last real run tomorrow. On Thursday we jog the course. Three days to go."

The clouds along the horizon had crept upwards, Kit saw as he walked home. The sky was paler. Autumn was coming, all right. Autumn or . . . something.

They'd almost finished dinner that night when Uncle Gil spoke. "Still working on contact with your folks, Kitt."

"Try not to worry," Aunt Fran added. Kit noticed suddenly how tired she and Uncle Gil looked. "These things take time."

Kit remembered Alrika talking about her mother and her mother's boyfriend. As surely as if a great searchlight had switched on inside his head, he understood that his mum and dad both loved him, and always would. The anger he'd felt at them vanished from his mind.

That night in his bedroom, in the house of two kind, half-known people, he moved around touching things once more. Then for only the second time, he lay on his bed and cried silently.

Twenty-one

Wednesday lunchtime. Six figures stretched sides and hamstrings, did shoulder loosening and back-bending. Then they spent training being silly.

"Forget about Friday," urged Ms. Gorton. "Enjoy yourselves."

So they did ballet jumps. Streve and Connell glanced nervously towards the school in case any guys were watching, then stopped glancing as they found ballet jumps were hard.

They sprinted facing forward, then facing backwards when Ms. Gorton called. Connell, busy joking about teachers who kept changing their minds, missed one call and ended up fifty metres away, still heading in the wrong direction. Even Alrika smiled.

They ran relays in different pairs. Alrika and Connell won; Hanni and Kit were a distant third. Then they ran relays in their own pairs. This time Alrika and Kit won—or rather, Alrika did, her long legs overtaking the other two girls.

They played tag. Streve let Hanni catch him easily. Alrika wouldn't let anyone catch her; she dodged and twisted till Mara tagged her with a sudden sprint.

Afterwards, they stood panting and grinning at one another. Then Ms. Gorton shooed them into the gym to put on track tops and jerseys.

"OK," she said, when all six were sitting down. "The next few days. No—the next *two* days." She paused, while people swallowed and Connell pretended to hide under his chair.

"Tomorrow we walk the course and just think. Tomorrow night, you're in bed by *nine o'clock*, OK? Don't worry if you can't sleep. Just lie and relax your muscles. That's what matters."

"A good breakfast on Friday. Bread, cornflakes, sugar or honey—heaps of carbohydrates. Drink about 300 millilitres of water an hour before the race. Maybe nibble a chocolate cookie during first lesson— I've told your teachers!"

She smiled, then looked serious again. "Come to the gym as soon as first lesson is over. And check your gear the night before. Make sure it's clean and comfortable."

A pause. "Any questions? OK, we'll walk and talk that course tomorrow. And please—nobody fall over a cliff between now and Friday."

"You'll have plenty on your mind for the next couple of days." Uncle Gil patted Kit on the shoulder that evening. "We're here if you need us."

Aunt Fran smiled agreement. I owe these two, Kit knew.

That night, he half woke and heard the rhythmic beeping sound. It was quiet, almost comforting. He could still hear it as he drifted back down to sleep.

They walked the cross-country course on Thursday lunchtime.

"Imagine tomorrow," Ms. Gorton said as they started down the first slope. "Some of Rygel will take off with a rush. You don't, Connell, OK? Keep them in sight, but don't burn out early. Streve, you and Hanni don't get *too* far behind. Push yourselves a bit."

They made their way through the first pines, noting again where the path was narrow and they mustn't be squeezed to the back. They crossed the streams on the big stones, Hanni almost slipping on one, Alrika grabbing her hand. They stood on the far bank.

"That's where you go for it." Their coach's face was tight. "You'll be tired, but you take off here— straight through the water."

They walked on, along the gravel road towards the paddocks. A breeze blew some of Alrika's hair across her face.

"You have to be ahead here," Ms. Gorton reminded them. "Remember Marec's big finish. And remember you *all* count—every person affects the result."

At the bottom of the final slope, they stopped.

"You know what this bit means." Ms. Gorton spoke quietly. "You know how you'll be feeling.

Chapter Twenty-one

But everyone in the team puts their head down and gives it all they've got."

She looked around the set faces. "You *are* a team. And I'm proud to be your coach."

Six pairs of eyes kept staring at the hill. Again Kit thought of the slope up to his parents' house. It didn't seem so important now.

He saw where he'd struggled or sprinted up so many times already. The steepest bits, the parts where grass clumps gave a good foothold. He saw himself charging up, Alrika right behind him.

The girl stood nearby. Her gaze too was fixed on the hill. Then she turned. For five seconds, they looked at each other in silence. There was no need for words.

Kit walked home with Streve after school. They said little.

"Thought it might rain tomorrow," the other boy muttered. "Looks like we'll be OK, but . . . "

Kit had forgotten the clouds. Now he saw them lying along the horizon, exactly as they'd lain for the last four days. Maybe a bit darker, but otherwise the same. Just ordinary clouds.

Twenty-two

Aunt Fran helped him check his gear on Thursday evening. "We wondered what it would be like to have someone running in a race like this," she said, then hugged Kit suddenly. "Now we know."

In his room later, he picked up Miss Garden's astronomy book for the first time since Saturday. He'd been too busy; other things were more important now.

The sentence he'd read a whole world ago seemed to shine out at him. *Some huge shock, and you could break into one of these parallel universes.*

For a minute, Kit felt as if all the breath had been squeezed from him. Tomorrow—the word beat in his mind. Tomorrow.

He expected to lie awake for hours. Instead he found himself floating through dreams where people were everywhere. His parents talked to Uncle Gil and Aunt Fran. Ms. Gorton stood beside Miss Garden. Streve, Hanni, and the others came and went. It was like a procession. He didn't see Alrika.

A few times, voices murmured. Once or twice the beeping noise grew, then faded. It was all very peaceful.

At Friday breakfast (two bowls of cornflakes and milk, three pieces of toast with honey) neither of his host parents said much.

Aunt Fran hugged him again when he was ready to leave. "Good luck, Kitt. We'll be there watching."

Uncle Gil began stretching out his hand, then hugged Kit, too. "Yes. Good luck, son—for everything."

Streve didn't say much on the way to school, either. He kept licking his lips, and jumped as a passing car tooted a greeting.

When they were nearly at the front gate, he spoke quietly. "Awesome to have you in the team, Kitt."

Kit's throat felt tight and his eyes prickled. But warmth glowed inside him.

"We wish our cross-country team the very best for today." Mrs. Hedley's smile moved from Kit to the other team members sitting silently in assembly. Mara's knees kept twitching. Streve and Connell kept yawning. Hanni and Alrika were still.

On the way to science, Kit passed through what sounded like a stuck CD. "Good luck, you guys. Show 'em, Kitt. Good luck." The warmth glowed again.

Mr. Nasser grinned at the nervous faces scattered around his room. "I've found how you can win today for sure. Get a metre in front of Rygel in the first minute, and they'll never catch you."

The nervous faces became gaping faces. Mr. Nasser grinned again. "Simple. By the time Rygel run that metre, you'll have run another half-metre. By the time they run that half-metre, you'll have run a quarter-metre. The distance between you gets smaller, but they never catch you. Works perfectly in science; dunno about the real world. Sorry."

Laughter and applause through the classroom. Hanni managed a smile around her water bottle. Streve managed one around his chocolate cookie. Alrika kept her eyes on her book.

Spectators were already arriving as Kit and the others headed for the gym. One group carried a banner: RYGEL RULES!

"Rygel sucks," muttered Connell—quietly.

The boys' changing room smelt of running shoes. Three faces turned to look as Kit, Streve, and Connell entered. The Rygel team, already in black shorts and red track tops.

Marec nodded. "Hi." Behind him, a long, thin boy about Kit's size and a small, chunky boy watched.

Connell and Streve mumbled replies. Kit looked at the broad-shouldered boy opposite. "Good luck, eh?"

"Thanks. You guys, too." Marec hesitated, glanced at Kit again. Then he and the other Rygel boys headed for the door. Cheers greeted them.

The Macmillan boys changed into their white shorts and green singlets. Kit and Streve were silent. Connell tried to crack a joke, muttered, "Hell, I gotta pee," and said nothing more.

They came out of the gym and stopped. The sports field was crammed with people.

The whole of Macmillan School was there. So were more Rygel supporters. Heaps of other people, too—Kit glimpsed Aunt Fran and Uncle Gil. He saw Mrs. Hedley talking to a group of men and women in suits. The sponsors?

The three boys joined an equally silent Hanni, Mara, and Alrika. For five minutes, they stretched muscles from neck to ankle. Kit could feel the concentration radiating from the others like heat.

When he finally looked up, he saw the start line was marked with flags on poles. Other flags led towards the first slope. Two people in track suits held clipboards as they chatted.

He saw the other Rygel kids, too, jogging on the far side of the field. Two of their girls were tall and longhaired, just like the girls he didn't dare speak to at his other school. The third, trotting beside Marec, was slightly shorter. Her running shoes looked new and expensive.

"Five minutes, runners!" called one of the track-suited figures.

"OK, people. Let's have you." Ms. Gorton spoke quietly.

The Macmillan team moved to where their coach stood. Kit's stomach churned, his legs trembled. But his mind was calm. Even the light around him seemed sharper. He would give the next half-hour everything he had. After that? *After that* could wait.

Ms. Gorton smiled at her team. "I want you to enjoy today. You're going to remember it for a very long time. Like I said, I'm proud of you."

"Two minutes!" came the call from the start line.

Ms. Gorton hugged the six twitching figures in turn. "These are your friends. Run for them!"

Streve, Connell, and Kit shook hands—sweaty hands, Kit noted. Then, before he realised what was happening, Mara and Hanni hugged him. The first time I've been hugged by a real girl! Kit thought. Pity we didn't do more of it in training.

Alrika was standing in front of him. She reached out and held both Kit's hands—hard. Her green eyes were fierce.

"That time I blacked out. It was like the dream I've had of falling. I was hurt. So were you. There was something enor—"

As Kit stared, the girl stopped and tried to smile. "I'll tell you more after we win—partner."

"All runners!" a voice called. "All runners to the start, please."

• • • • • • • • • • • • • • • • •

They formed up at the line. Six red singlets, six green singlets. They licked lips and shuffled feet. Nobody spoke. A track-suited figure stood holding a flag. The crowd were silent.

I'm sweating already, Kit knew. Alrika's words lay in a far corner of his mind. He'd think about it later, after . . . after.

"We're gonna get wet," Streve mumbled beside him.

Kit looked up. The clouds had left the distant hills and spread halfway across the sky. Great silent towers in black and purple that seemed to drain the light from around them.

A second only, then—"Ready, everyone?" Kit jerked his head down, and saw the official lift his flag.

"Go!" The flag dropped, and they were running.

Twenty-three

The crowd exploded. "Rygel RULES! Rygel RULES!" rose and vanished under shouts of "Mac-MILLAN! Mac-MILLAN!" Other voices yelled "Go, Kitt!" The familiar double *t* snapped in his ear.

Over the edge of the sports field they went, onto the downward slope. A sudden wind gust cuffed them, made Hanni stagger.

Spectators packed the slope, too. Kit glimpsed Aunt Fran and Uncle Gil again, silent among the yelling crowd. His host mother smiled. Uncle Gil lifted one hand in what might have been a greeting or a farewell. Kit had no time to think; as he strode downwards, the wind blew again, harder. He lowered his head and pushed on.

The cheering voices faded behind. Thudding feet and heavy breathing took over. Four Rygel runners—the two tall girls, plus the skinny and chunky guys—had already shot ahead. Behind them, Marec and his partner ran steadily. Macmillan were clumped together in the rear.

More flags on posts marked the course towards the first pines. Another track-suited official stood beside them. This is big-time! Kit realised.

"Wait!" called Mara, as Connell started to race after the Rygel leaders. "Keep—up!" Hanni urged Streve.

Alrika was silent. She's already said plenty, Kit thought. He recalled her words a few moments back, and a rush of amazement sent him surging forward. Now Alrika spoke. "Not yet!"

The pine tops bowed in the wind. Their branches turned the day to dusk.

"Stay close!" Kit panted. The others quickened their pace; next moment, all six Macmillan runners were bunched behind Marec and his partner. The other four Rygel runners were at least twenty metres ahead.

Deeper into the pines they ran, past another official. The shorter Rygel girl's new shoes shone in the gloom. A couple of times, Marec glanced over his shoulder. He wants to be at the back, Kit knew. He doesn't like having us right behind him.

He watched the couple ahead. Marec and his partner strode on smoothly. They've got lots in reserve, Kit thought. And so have we! His teammates' determination seemed to crackle around him. Ms. Gorton was only half right—he wasn't *ever* going to forget this!

The light when they burst out of the pines didn't seem much brighter. But Kit hardly noticed. The other four Rygel runners were just ten metres in front. They were slowing down.

. . . .

Now the two streams lay ahead. Kit saw the first Rygel pair hesitate, then head for a shallower part. The next two red singlets moved towards a different stretch of bank.

Marec called out. Kit couldn't hear the words, but he sensed the annoyance in the boy's voice. At the same moment, a different voice hissed in his ear. "Straight! Straight through!"

Even as she spoke, Alrika swept past him, elbows pumping as she aimed at the near bank. The other green singlets clumped behind her. Kit saw the strain on Hanni's and Mara's faces; heard Streve grunting "Keep together!"

They ploughed through the hip-deep water. Spray flew; feet sloshed and squelched as they scrambled up the far bank. Breath was rasping in lungs now. Legs were hurting.

Alrika didn't slow for an instant. She charged into the second stream. Her long legs drove through the water. Her bony jaw was clenched.

No way am I gonna tell her to relax today, thought Kit. She is . . . *awesome!*

The streams so far had taken thirty seconds. In those seconds, they'd gained twenty metres lead on Rygel.

Excitement gripped Kit again. This was exactly what Ms. Gorton had wanted. He could hear Rygel yelling to one another behind. Now the other school had to catch them. Now Marec would need every bit of his famous finish.

* * * * * * * * * * * * * * * * * *

The second stream's bank lay just ahead. Alrika was already scrambling from the water, slipping on the smooth grey stones.

As Kit began to follow, a dark shadow swooped over him. Without thinking, he stared upwards.

The sky overhead was crammed with giant clouds. Clouds exactly like the ones towering over Jackson Road that Sunday two weeks or two universes ago. They rolled and poured forward like some great avalanche. Out of the middle of them, a huge black circle swelled.

Behind Kit, Streve yelled. "Watch ou—"

Too late. Kit's left foot skidded on the wet stone. His legs flew from beneath him, and he crashed down. The side of his head cracked against the rock where Alrika's footprints still glistened.

Twenty-four

He was up again instantly, shaking his head, saying a word he usually said under his breath.

"Kitt!" Hanni's voice. "You all right?"

Streve and Connell had him by the arms, hauling him up the far bank. Kit's legs kept moving, stumbling forward when the boys let him go. His face was wet; he must have gone right into the water. He held one hand against the side of his head, and blinked as the hand came away streaked with blood.

"Kitt!" It was Mara this time. "You better stop."

Then a pale, bony face was right in front of him, green eyes glaring. It was so much like his dream that Kit gaped.

"Can you run?" Alrika's voice was a hiss. "Can you?"

"Yeah." Kit heard himself mumble. "Yeah. I—"

"Then do it!" The green eyes blazed. "Run!"

He ran. His legs were already moving, driving towards the gravel road. The side of his head felt thick and hot; blood slid down his cheek and neck. But he was running.

Rygel had just started to cross the second stream. He'd glimpsed them as Streve and Connell half-dragged him up the bank. Marec and his partner were in the lead.

"You OK, son?" an official called as they reached the gravel road.

"Yes!" It was Alrika. Then they were pounding along the road.

The ground beneath his feet was dark. The rough grass and scrub beside the road seemed dark, too. Kit knew it was the clouds, piling and massing above.

He kept his head down, watching his skinny legs thrust forward. He heard Alrika, panting beside him. His own breath sounded distant.

The other four Macmillan runners had fallen behind. Their thudding feet were fainter. He and Alrika charged along. We have to keep our lead, Kit told himself. We have to keep ahead of Marec.

"Go!" Alrika hissed again in his ear. "Go, Kit! Run!"

They plunged into the second lot of pines. The world darkened still more around them. Wind moaned and thrashed in the treetops.

Out of the pines and across the paddocks. Alrika sped along at Kit's elbow. Her coppery-red hair streamed in the wind. It was like running beside a flame. Her long lean body flowed forward. Her eyes darted sideways to watch him. A great silence seemed to surround them.

103

The side of Kit's head still felt thick and muzzy. But the blood had stopped trickling down his face and neck.

The silence was broken by the thud of feet. Two pairs of feet, behind them. Kit didn't look round; he knew who it was. Marec and his partner. Marec, winding up for his big finish, catching them already.

Now Kit could glimpse the red singlets from the corner of his eye. He tried to go harder, then staggered as dizziness swept him.

Straight away, Alrika swerved till her shoulder was touching his. "Hold on!" she grunted. "Kit! Hold on!"

The words thundered in Kit's mind. Suddenly his head was clear again. He looked ahead, and there was the final slope.

A line of flags led straight up towards the sports field and the finish. Another official stood near the bottom. At the top of the slope, Kit saw the roof of . . . his parents' house? No, the gym; it must be the gym. Black cloud-towers loomed above it.

He took it all in with one glance. He had no time for any more, because suddenly Marec was past him.

The broad-shouldered Rygel boy stared at Kit's blood-smeared head. The Rygel girl beside him panted and struggled to keep up. But she was already dropping back as the slope began to rise.

"Go! Please—Kit!" Even as Alrika gasped, Kit somehow found new strength. In five steps, he and Alrika surged past the Rygel girl. Legs thrust, arms pumped as they pushed up the slope, behind Marec.

The crowd at the top roared encouragement. The noise swept down at Kit and Alrika, mixed with another roaring that seemed to come from the sky itself.

And suddenly Kit saw that Marec was tiring. The shoulders in the red singlet moved jerkily. The feet slipped as they struggled upwards.

The top of the slope drew closer. The crowd roar was deafening. Voices yelled, arms waved, faces stared.

Kit glimpsed Aunt Fran and Uncle Gil, watching gravely. Ms. Gorton—or was it Miss Garden? Mr. Nasser; no, Mr. Harris. Sweat stung his eyes. His whole body was one racking ache for air. Fresh blood slid down his face.

Two other faces stared at him, and the rest of the crowd blurred. His mum and dad? It couldn't be. It was.

An enormous power flooded Kit's body. His skin prickled and tingled.

He hurled himself forward, past the exhausted Marec. The other boy's startled, gaping mouth brought back another race, in another time. Above him, he sensed a gigantic black opening swooping downward. The roar of the crowd became a roaring engine. Their screaming voices were like a horn blaring.

Then he was flinging himself over the finish line, a full metre ahead of Marec. He sensed Alrika diving across too, falling heavily just behind him. He tried to gasp her name, but the world had dropped away into nothingness under him. He went plunging, spiralling down into darkness.

Twenty-five

"Beep . . . beep . . . beep." That noise he'd heard at night. Kit tried to see what it was. But his whole body felt aching and weak. He groaned. "Alrika?" he began to say.

"Kit. Oh, Kit." The voice spoke his name with one *t*. He knew that voice.

A face was above him. It blurred, disappeared, came back. He knew that face, too. His mother. She was crying. Her eyes stared down at him.

Again, Kit tried to speak. "Mum?" It came out as a croak.

Another face appeared beside his mother's. His dad. His dad looking pale and exhausted.

"Hi, mate," his father said. "Welcome back."

Then his father was crying, too.

A different voice spoke. "Let's have a look at this young troublemaker."

Two more faces loomed above him. Aunt Fran and Uncle Gil! No, not quite. One of them held Kit's wrist. The other pushed aside some sort of machine. Kit glimpsed a dial, with a green line travelling across it and jumping at regular intervals. He heard the beeping noise. He saw that the two new figures wore white coats.

He was lying in a bed. His head felt thick. That's right; he'd hurt it against the river stone. But he'd won! He'd beaten Marec. He looked around for Alrika, and groaned again as his neck hurt.

His parents were smiling now. Smiling and still crying. How weird, Kit began to think. Then soft darkness swelled up around him.

Time passed. He lay while people came and went. Some time after that, his eyes were open again.

Hey, he was at school. Macmillan School—the name was there on the wall.

No. *Macmillan Ward*, the sign said. *Opened 1994*. Kit lay staring. Deep down, he began to understand.

He shifted his head carefully. Green curtains surrounded his bed. On the ceiling, light from somewhere outside threw patterns like clouds moving.

The curtains opened, the clouds disappeared, and the Aunt Fran woman stood by his bed in her white coat. She took his wrist again; smiled down at him. "Well, young Kitt. You've given everyone a fright, haven't you?"

"Wha—" Kit began. The doctor—he knew she was a doctor—raised one hand.

"You're going to be OK. That's the main thing. Twenty-eight stitches in your head; they make hard fence posts on Jackson Road. Cuts and bruises, but they've had time to heal. No brain damage, Kitt. Got that? No brain damage."

"No brain," Kit managed to whisper.

The woman smiled again. Her voice sounded slightly foreign; she pronounced his name with a double *t*. "Great to have you back with us, Kitt. You've certainly been in a world of your own."

He was skinny. He could feel it when he moved his arms or legs. He'd lost heaps of weight.

His parents were sitting beside his bed again. His mother seemed to guess what was in his mind.

"The hospital had you on a drip, but you . . . you were fading away." Her mouth trembled. Kit's father put his arm around her, and she went on.

"Then a week ago, your body seemed to decide to live. You began taking on lots of fluid. That's— that's when we started to hope." And his mother cried and smiled once more.

Through a nearby window, Kit could see an elevated walkway leading to the next block. It reminded him of something; he tried to think what.

The afternoon sunlight had almost gone from Macmillan Ward before he knew. It was the steel bridge that had appeared on Jackson/Jakson Road.

It all happened here, he told himself. In this place. In my mind and my dreams. It all happened here.

• • • • • • • • • • • • • • • • •

"Almost three weeks," the Uncle Gil doctor told him next morning. Dr. Gilbert—and the woman's nametag read Dr. Francovic.

"Your mum and dad have been here all the time," Dr. Francovic told him now. "They must have the hardest bottoms in the world. They just sat by your bed, saying *Hold on. Hold on.* Plus they had us telling you they were trying to get through."

"You should have made a tape," Kit murmured.

Dr. Gilbert grinned, then looked serious. "They brought you back, Kit. A couple of times, we thought we were going to lose you. You were fading away. Your mother and father sat there, pouring their lives into you. They did it, son."

Kit managed a nod. He knew the doctor was right. But in his mind was another voice and another face—a pale, bony face, with coppery hair and fierce green eyes. Where was that face now?

"You kept twitching your legs as if you were running, so the doctors knew your spine was OK." His dad sat by the bed, gripping Kit's hand. Another day had passed. Already, Kit felt stronger and clearer.

"And the brain scans showed you were thinking away like crazy," added his mother, who had an equally firm grip on Kit's other hand.

His father half-chuckled. "You started saying

something. Sounded like earache. You'd go *Earache*? Dr. Francovic reckoned it must be your sore head."

Kit was silent. After a moment, his dad said, "Mr. Taylor sends his best. He's thrilled to hear you're OK."

Kit stared. His mother sighed. "He says he'll never forget seeing you in the middle of the road, staring up like you were star-gazing or something."

Now Kit remembered—the truck tearing towards him, the bulky figure pulling at the wheel. He shuddered, and his father held his hand tighter.

"He knows he was driving too fast, son. He was hurrying to get some hay in before the storm broke. He's had a fright, too."

Two more days passed. Kit slept, sat up in bed for a while, slept again. Dr. Gilbert and Dr. Francovic came and went. His parents were there nearly all the time. There was no sign of the other figure Kit kept waiting for.

"Sorry," he told his mother and father, as another afternoon drew towards dusk. "Sorry for the trouble."

"We're sorry, too." His mum kissed his forehead.

"Sorry for all sorts of things," his dad added.

Kit watched them smile at each other. For a second, they looked exactly like Mara and Connell. They're friends now, he understood. They mightn't be together again, but they're friends.

· · · · · · · · · · · · · · · · · ·

"There's a card for you," his father told him next morning. Kit read the words he usually saw at Christmas. "Love from Auntie and Uncle." Another two names clicked into place.

"Lots of messages from people at the school," his dad went on. "Mr. Harris says the school cross-country team will go down on their knees if you'll join them. Miss Garden, Mr. Dudley—they all send their best."

"Kids, too," his mum added. "Steve Sutton and that little girlfriend of his—Hannah."

"Anyone else?" Kit asked after a moment.

"And Mark Taylor. They're coming to see you in a few days."

His parents left, smiling. Kit lay, watching the sign: MACMILLAN WARD.

Inside his head, he was saying goodbye. Alrika was gone. He didn't know where, but he knew he would never see the blazing green eyes, the bony, edgy face again.

And he knew he would never forget her.

Twenty-six

Kit healed quickly. After five days, he could sit in a chair in the sunroom. After a week, he could walk slowly along the corridor of Macmillan Ward. New patients came; old patients went. Green curtains went up around beds, then came down.

One morning, he flicked through the astronomy book that lay in his bedside locker. A name leaped out at him. *The massive blue-white star Rigel, 60,000 times as bright as our Sun* . . . Kit shook his head and put the book away again.

Mark Taylor's father visited. "Sorry, mate," the big man mumbled, as he stared at the bandages around Kit's head. "Mark was gonna come, too, but he's a bit scared of hospitals."

"No worries," Kit replied. He just might give Mark Taylor a few surprises when he was back at school.

"The doctors reckon it was amazing the way you held on," Mr. Taylor said. "Hell, you should be an Olympic long jumper, mate, the way you chucked yourself at the ditch. You saved your own life. You were incredible."

Ambulance sirens wailed that afternoon. The next morning, a dazed and pale-faced man lay three beds away.

Kit only half-noticed him. "The ward's name," he finally asked his dad. "Is it—"

"Macmillan is the big electronics firm outside town. They sponsor this place." His father looked pleased with himself. "I phoned them, told them how grateful we were for this ward. Their managing director said that helped make their minds up. They're keeping the sponsorship going and they may even increase it."

Dad, the big businessman, thought Kit. He'll never change.

The day after that, a familiar face smiled at Kit from the foot of his bed. Ms. Gorton! No, Miss Garden.

"Come to get my book back," she said. "Hope it answered a few things for you too?"

"It . . . yeah." Kit replied. "Yeah, I guess it did."

He was going home the next day. That afternoon, two more familiar faces appeared. Hannah Wesley and Steve Sutton walked into the sunroom where Kit sat.

"You look awesome!" Steve gazed at Kit's bandaged head.

"Heaps of kids from school say hi," pretty, fair-haired Hannah told Kit. "They were gonna come, but Mr. Dudley reckoned we should wait till you're back."

"Anyone new at school?" Kit tried to keep his voice casual.

"Nah." Hannah shook her head.

Kit watched them from the sunroom window as they walked down the drive. They were holding hands. Sudden loneliness stabbed him.

The man three beds away looked much better the next morning. More curtains, dappled with early sunlight, were up at the end of the ward. Kit had half-heard voices as he fell asleep.

"Some young guy. Not sure what happened to him." Kit's father beamed with happiness as he waited for his son. Kit's clothes felt heavy; his sneakers clumped when he walked.

Dr. Gilbert and Dr. Francovic were there to say goodbye. Kit's parents hugged them both; then it was his turn. As Dr. Gilbert shook his hand, Kit saw a worried-looking woman emerge from behind the green curtains at the far end.

"Take it easy at school, young Kitt." Dr. Francovic kissed him on the cheek. "You'll have a new classmate in a few weeks, when she recovers." As Kit stared, Dr. Francovic nodded at the far curtains. "Poor kid; she's been away with the fairies half the night."

"She? I thought it was a boy," said Kit's mother.

Dr. Gilbert shook his head. "A girl. Bit of an athlete; nasty fall on a training run." He turned to Kit's parents. "She and her mother have just moved here. A new start, I think."

Kit's voice felt clogged in his throat. "What's her name?"

Dr. Gilbert looked amused. "Erica. Why?"

Erica.

"Can you wait a second?" Kit ignored his parents' surprised looks. At the end of the ward, he paused by the curtains. His heart thudded; his mouth was dry.

"Hello?" he managed to say. A voice on the other side murmured something. Kit opened the curtains and stepped through.

His first feeling was disappointment. Sunlight striking between the curtains made him squint, but he could see that the girl lying in bed had short brown hair. One side of her face was bruised and swollen. Her left arm was bandaged.

The eyes staring at him in surprise were green, though. And as Kit looked, hope and disbelief started to churn inside him.

The girl was still staring. Kit suddenly felt awkward. "I—I'm going home today. I've been here for a while. They're good. They really look after you."

The brown-haired girl relaxed slightly. "Thanks." Her voice was muffled still.

"Dr. Francovic—she says you're coming to our school."

The girl gave a half-shrug. She sounded clearer now. "Yeah. We just arrived. Been trying to get fit for this awesome cross-country team you've got. Dream on, eh?"

Kit swallowed. He knew that voice! "You'll be OK," he managed to say. "Dreams can come true. Can't they?"

The girl's breath jerked. Her eyes locked with Kit's. I'm really looking at a girl, a corner of his mind rejoiced. He swallowed again, took a deep breath, and made himself speak once more.

"You just . . . just hold on."

Absolute silence. The girl didn't move. Understanding and amazement filled her eyes.

Kit nodded. "That's all," he said again. "You hold on."

Now she smiled. Her face changed. As she moved her head on the pillow, a blaze of sunlight turned her brown hair coppery-red. With a great surge of joy, Kit knew he'd been right.

"I will," she told him. "I'll hold on. See you at school, then?"

"Yeah." Kit smiled back. "See you at school. I can show you some training places, if you like." And he added, for the first time, "Erica."

Then he went out into the main part of the ward, into his world where his mum and dad stood close together, talking quietly to each other.